Them O

Astor

Book 1 of Them Old Bones Hexalogy

Them Old Bones, Book 1 of 6 in the book series Them Old Bones Hexalogy

By Astor Y Teller

Copyright © 2023 by Astor Y Teller.

Artwork by Astor Y Teller

All rights reserved. This book or any portion thereof may not be reproduced or used in any manner without the express written permission of the author, except for the use of brief quotations in a book review.

This is a work of fiction. Names, characters, businesses, places, events and incidents are either the products of the author's imagination or used in a fictitious manner.

ISBN: 9798854585453

To M

And ubiquitous thanks to Torgrim Mellum Stene and Elaine Newman who strolled and picked their way through my universe (along with the friendly troupe of vanguard readers)

Based on a true story[1]

---

[1] According to Vault Master Cerrakin the world doesn't consist of stories, but realities do. Realities are nothing but the stories which we use to make sense of the world (our senses don't do that part, they just stick to the registering part). And this story is part of a reality that I walked into and wrote down as it approached and suffused me. I didn't make it up. After all, I'm a storyteller, not a storymaker. And this story is just as true as money is true and borders are true and religion is true and Santa is true. Just ask Cerrakin.

Part 1: To pick a bone — 8
    Chapter 1 — 9
    Chapter 2 — 11
    Chapter 3 — 13
    Chapter 4 — 15
    Chapter 5 — 18
    Chapter 6 — 20
    Chapter 7 — 22
    Chapter 8 — 26
    Chapter 9 — 30
    Chapter 10 — 35
    Chapter 11 — 39

Interlude: A lesson in world building — 42
    Chapter 12 — 42

Part 2: Vaulting with Crazyjones — 48
    Chapter 13 — 48
    Chapter 14 — 51
    Chapter 15 — 55
    Chapter 16 — 58
    Chapter 17 — 62
    Chapter 18 — 65
    Chapter 19 — 69
    Chapter 20 — 72
    Chapter 21 — 75
    Chapter 22 — 79
    Chapter 23 — 82
    Chapter 24 — 86
    Chapter 25 — 88
    Chapter 26 — 91
    Chapter 27 — 94
    Chapter 28 — 98

Chapter 29	101
Chapter 30	104
Chapter 31	107
Chapter 32	110
Chapter 33	112
Chapter 34	115
Chapter 35	119
Part 3: Countdown with Miriam	**123**
Chapter 36	123
Chapter 37	126
Chapter 38	129
Chapter 39	134
Chapter 40	136
Chapter 41	142
Chapter 42	145
Chapter 43	149
Chapter 44	152
Chapter 45	158
Chapter 46	161
Chapter 47	163
Epilogue:	**165**
Chapter 48	165
Peek: A few days into the future	**168**
Chapter 49	168
Cast (alphabetically)	**172**

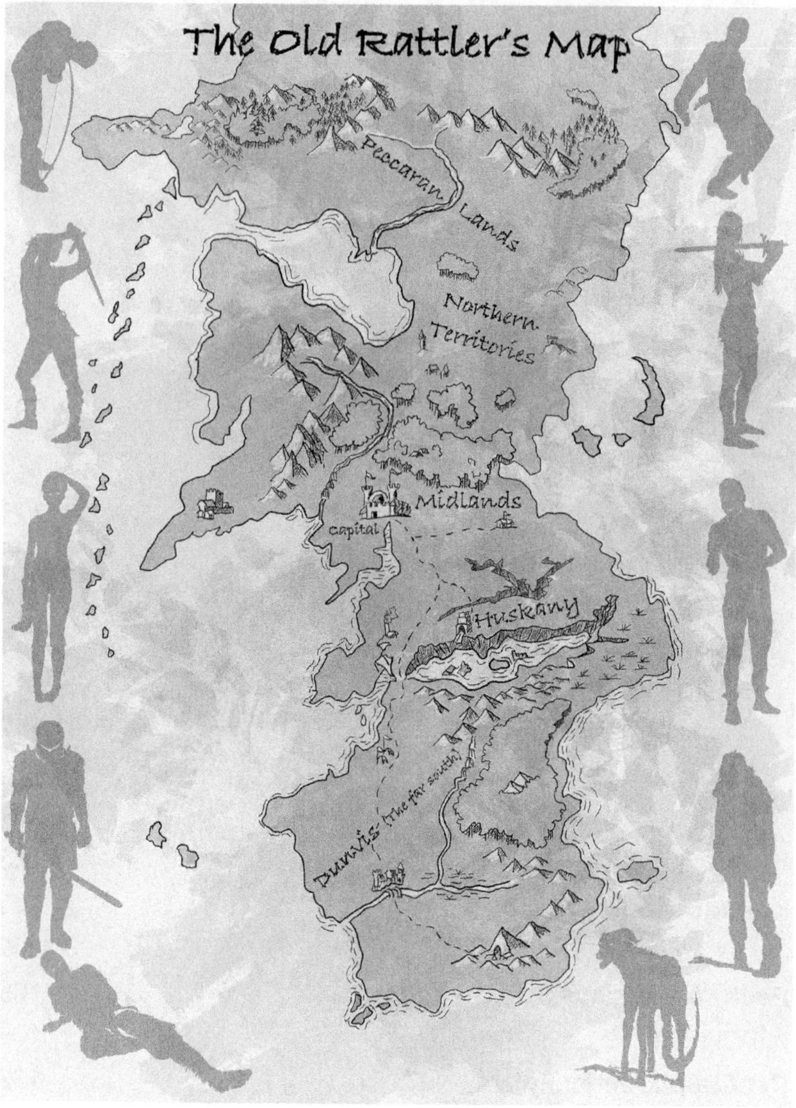
The Old Rattler's Map
Peccaran Lands
Northern Territories
Midlands
capital
Huskany
Dunvis (The far south)

Part 1: To pick a bone
Chapter 1

People call me a bone collector, but in truth I am not. Anyone can collect bones, like the farmer I am meeting today. He is waiting in the shade of an old gnarled oak, sitting with his back against the mossy trunk, but when he sees me he is quick on his feet, supporting himself with something big and long that I expect he will hand over to me soon.

"You are the bone collector, eh?" he asks.

I don't bother to correct him, so I nod. I walked a long way to get here, and would rather leave out the chit-chat so I can get back home as soon as possible.

The farmer assesses me, while I take a peek at him as well. He is a lanky fellow with unruly hair and a light beard, wearing a threadbare motley jacket that could have passed for a jester's jacket in a poor man's court.

I guess that my dark clothes could make me pass for a brigand, and my scowl is probably not helping, since the farmer doesn't approach me, but is still doing his assessing.

"Or did the neighbour call you out to pester me?" the farmer asks straightforwardly.

"Excuse me?"

"You bone collectors might not have that problem," the farmer says, scratching his beard with a chapped hand. "Neighbours, I mean. They are even worse than the rats in the barn if you ask me."

The farmer has obviously started the chit-chat without my approval. I came here for a bone, not rural stupidity.

I take a closer look at the bone he is leaning on and see now that it is a hoe.

Where the hell is that bone?

He must feel my temper flare up because he stops leaning on the hoe and shifts it into his hands in what he thinks must be a casual way.

"Well, I didn't call you out here," the farmer says, partly as an excuse but with a hint of humour. "And the dog most certainly did not."

"What dog?"

"My dog. The neighbour always complains about my dog. Last week—"

I turn my back to leave, before I burst with anger. This must be a misunderstanding, but to understand the error, I have to go back to the city and take a look in The Vault, where all the messages are kept together with all the unearthed writings and the bones from the old, the elder and the eldest times.

Or maybe one of my stupid colleagues is pulling my leg.

My sour mood moulds and leaves a sticky taste in my mouth.

"Leaving already?" the farmer asks behind my back.

I turn around slowly.

"Well, I didn't come here for tea," I say and give him my cool stare.

"No, apparently you came for the bone."

"So you do have a bone?"

"No. My dog has it. He dug it up in the neighbour's field." The farmer takes stock of me and decides that I'm worth a gossip, even with a temper. "I do have tea if you are interested."

"What about coffee?" I ask.

The farmer nods and puts the hoe on his shoulder and turns to walk.

"Follow me," he says.

He has a lazy gait, so it would be easy to keep apace with him, but I decide to walk behind him, like a skulking brigand, for I'm not in a friendly mood.

I hope the coffee can remedy that.

Chapter 2

With me in tow, the farmer detours from the road and onto a dirt track that sticks to the shade under the canopy. We pass the outskirts of a hamlet and scare off a flock of grazing sheep on a meadow before we enter a clearing with a saggy-roofed cottage in the centre of it.

"Here we are," the farmer says and gives me a smile.

He opens the door for me and I walk inside.

The house has seen better days. Apart from the new looking hole in the roof, everything else is in a ramshackle state.

Like a discarded sock with a brand new hole, I think to myself.

An old bucket collects water and sunlight under the roof hole. The rest of the room is wrapped in shadows. I try to look out of the nearest window while the farmer goes over to the kitchen to brew some tea, but I can see that the flies died trying. They lie feet up on the window sills, coated in so much old dust that they look furried.

Apparently Mr. Farmer is not married, except to the hoe that he brought with him into the kitchen. He must be one of those lonely guys. That explains the dog.

"Do you need help," I hear my better self ask loudly.

"I'm fine, thanks. You find a seat near the hole. There should be a chair nearby."

Well, I can't see it, so I settle on an old chest and wait a few minutes. The farmer returns from the kitchen with a tray with two steaming cups and looks quizzically at me.

"What's wrong?" I ask.

"You're sitting on the table."

"Oh? I'm sorry." I get up from the chest lid and he puts the tray down, before he brings out two sandwiched chairs from the shadows. He takes the top one which is upside down, turns it the right way and places it in front of me to sit down on.

I sit down.

So does he. He hands me one of the cups and I drink and try to not think of the bone I was here to collect, so I can keep myself from getting angry and naughty and giving me and my colleagues a bad reputation. I already have too many complaints on my back.

"It's too hot for me," the farmer says, "I have to wait."

"I don't like to wait."

"I can see that."

"I would have fixed the hole in the roof a lifetime ago," I say.

"No, you wouldn't," the farmer says and looks up at the hole. "I made it last month."

"You made it?"

"Yup. It gives me both water and light."

I'm too stunned to reply. I look at him and think he must be an idiot.

"You think I'm an idiot," he says with a hint of a smile.

"I'm here to collect a dead bone, not to judge the living."

"So you truly are dead."

I hate it when people remind me of that and take a sip of the scolding coffee that is, in fact, tea and doesn't taste anything but old memories of tea. I wanted coffee to access my good coffee memories, so I could be a little more friendly. As I look up to consider reminding him that I requested coffee, he studies me like I am some kind of funny freak.

The farmer leans forward and looks closer at me. "You don't feel it, do you?"

"The tea?"

"The hotness of it. And other things. Like the thingy between your legs, does it still responds to stimulus?"

"It's a hole."

"Makes sense. Why keep the deadwood, when it can rot away? I guess you still have the memories of tumbling with the girlies."

"I said a hole."

He ponders on that for a few seconds. Then it dawns on him. "Like a girly hole?"

I nod. "Anything else you would like to know?"

But the farmer is too busy turning red.

Chapter 3

"I'm sorry," is his excuse before he runs back to the kitchen and leaves me sitting in the dark. When he comes back, it is with a new steaming cup. He puts it on my side of the chest.

"Coffee, as you requested, Miss Bone Collector," he says in his most dignified way. He has chosen to postpone the girly hole and thingy business indefinitely, although I can sense that he suddenly wants to play gentleman and make an impression, so I play along and listen to his excuses. "I'm sorry that I forgot that you asked for coffee and gave you tea instead."

"No harm done." I take a sip of the new cup which brings me pleasant memories of good strong coffee.

"Miss Bone Collector liked it?"

"Very much, thank you. You can call me Miriam, by the way."

"I'm Crazyjones."

That doesn't surprise me one bit.

"May I enquire where your dog is?"

"He is up and around," the farmer says. "He is definitely not here."

"In the dog house then?"

"No, I mean he is not here, because he hasn't greeted you. Tenderloin is a polite dog, always making new acquaintances wherever he roams."

"Tenderloin?"

"My dog."

"Funny name."

"He doesn't take offence, since he neither talks nor listens."

"And his new acquaintance? The bone?"

"Do you mind if I drink the rest of your tea?" Crazyjones asks out of the blue.

"Be my guest."

He leans into the circle of light emanating from the hole in the roof and takes the tea cup from the chest, leans back into shadow, gulps it down and puts the empty cup back on the chest again.

"That was fast," I say.

"The warm part is the best part. It would be a shame to let it get lukewarm and then grow cold and become an insult to the kindling that heated it."

I nod and decide that Crazyjones definitely must be as crazy as the name implies.

"Should we look for Tenderloin?" I ask.

"Why?"

"To find the bone."

"He doesn't have it."

"What?" I sweep my courtesy under the rug. My icy stare makes him cringe. "So why am I in this shithole?"

"To get the bone? Or do you suddenly want the dog? Is that why the neighbour called on you? You are a dog catcher?"

"No. I want the bone. And then I want to leave."

"Okay," says Crazyjones and picks up his hoe. "Let's go out and get it then."

"You know where it is?"

"I have an inkling. And with the help of Juicycrunch we will probably find it."

"Is that your neighbour?"

"No, it's my hoe and he likes to dig, just like Tenderloin." Crazyjones stands up. "Let's go out and unearth the bone," he says to his hoe. Then he turns to me. "You are welcome to join us."

Chapter 4

We walk along the side of a field that has newly been plowed. The earth is still moist and black in the furrows.

"Did you find the bone here?" I ask.

Crazyjones turns around and shakes his head. "No. This is my field. Tenderloin likes to keep as far away as he can from it."

"Why?"

"Because he has bad memories from this field." Then Crazyjones smiles apologetically. "I strapped him to the plow to get my field done."

"He must be a big dog then."

"More strong than big. And he owes me."

"How so?"

"Tenderloin killed the plow horse. It was an accident, he assured me, so –"

"He assured you?" I interrupt.

"Yup, in a doggy way. That is why he lets me use him for plowing, but every time he gives me that sad doggy stare."

I thank him for the information in a polite way and hurry him along. This becomes more and more awkward. I want the bone and then to go home.

I might be dead, but that doesn't mean that I like the strange and eerie.

We leave the field and follow the tracks through a forest. Apart from some birds high above us, it is hauntingly quiet and dark as twilight.

As we walk, I get a distinct feeling of being watched.

I pretend not to notice, and engage Crazyjones in conversation. While he rambles about everything that comes to his mind and I answer with random yesses, noes and hmpfs, I let my eyes scan the area.

"So why is this bone picking so important?" Crazyjones says without turning around. "Is it for your collection?"

"No."

"Is it because bones out in the wilderness could be haunted?"

"Hmpf."

"I get it, you can't tell me. Guild secrets."

"Yes…" Then I spy movement to my left.

Something big and dark with reddish eyes comes out from the trees, amazingly silent when you consider the size, which is close to a horse.

I whisper to Crazyjones: "We are being followed. Don't turn around while I unsheathe my sword."

But the stupid bugger turns around and looks first at me, then towards what I'm looking at, before finally breathing a sigh of relief.

"You scared me, Miriam. I thought it was the neighbour."

"It's something far worse," I say and look at the emberglowing eyes and the big dark body a few strides away. I cannot make out whether it is fur or spikes that are sticking out of the body.

When I unsheathe my sword the monster snarls and shows a row of white sharp teeth.

"Sheathe your sword, Miriam," Crazyjones says in a most casual way. "It is only Tenderloin. He won't bite unless provoked."

"That is no ordinary dog."

"I take that as a compliment," Crazyjones says, swelling with pride. I never intended it as a compliment, but neither the monstrous dog nor Crazyjones seem to care.

I turn to Crazyjones while pointing the sword at the monsterdog. "And now you are going to tell me that your plough-horse provoked him?"

"To be honest, the horse wasn't mine. I borrowed it from the neighbour. And that stupid horse kicked Tenderloin first."

My sympathies go to the neighbour. I understand why the neighbour is angry with Crazyjones. People with monsters hanging around are never much liked. The same goes for The Vault in the city. The cityfolk compare me and my colleagues with monsters.

I toy with the idea of bringing Tenderloin home with me, to let the cityfolk behold a real monster.

"I think he is smiling at you," Crazyjones says. "Unless he is feeling threatened, that is."

I take the hint and sheathe my sword.

Tenderloin stops snarling and trots over to us. He is not as tall as a horse, but he is much broader. Crazyjones gives me something from his pouch – it is a rabbit's foot – and shoves me in front of the monster.

"Give him a snack and he will take a liking to you."

I put my hand out and close my eyes when the big snout sniffs loudly and the jaws open wide. I hear a crunch and loud chewing.

"Good boy!"

And when I open my eyes, my hand is still attached to my arm and the rabbit's foot has been swapped with monster dribble. Tenderloin snarls at me again and breathes moist and hot air from his snout.

"I think he really likes you," Crazyjones assures me. "You can tell by the way he smiles with his teeth."

"Those are not teeth, but fangs," I say.

I shouldn't have said the last bit, as Tenderloin growls like bad thunder.

"I'm sorry, I meant no offense," I say to the beast which is now standing on its hind legs.

"You are so dead," says the big bad beast towering over me.

Chapter 5

I assess the situation coolly. As I can't get my sword out in time, I use my tongue, addressing the big bad beast.

"Dead you say? Then we have something in common, Tenderloin."

The monster blinks his red eyes. Sudden confusion has jumped onto him and given me some time.

People don't talk with monsters; they scream or run away or act stupid and die. But he is back on his menacing track before I have a chance to do something stupid.

"We have nothing in common, little human."

"Yes we do," I say as calmly as I can, while thanking the hundreds of hours of hazardous courses in The Vault, being beaten and trapped and zapped, to truly know what I am. "We are both dead."

"We'll see about that," Tenderloin growls and opens his massive jaws. It's like looking into a shark's mouth. The shock of it snaps me out of my training and I close my eyes, something you should never do when you are dealing with monsters.

But the anticipated crunch of my body never arrives.

Instead I hear a loud juicy crunch and a yelp.

When I open my eyes the situation has turned around.

Tenderloin is sitting on the ground, rubbing his nose with his front paws, while looking at Crazyjones who is standing over him. To be exact, he is not looking at the farmer, but at the hoe that is raised above his head.

Juicycrunch?

Tenderloin is obviously afraid of Juicycrunch the hoe and I suspect he is also afraid of Crazyjones' temper.

They must be bonded in some way, all three of them. That would explain Crazyjones' apparent madness.

"Why did you hit me, master?"

"You said you couldn't talk!" Crazyjones raises Juicycrunch even higher above his head. "You lied to me!"

Well, that doesn't make sense – how can you lie if you can't speak –

but it does make sense in a way. Crazyjones must be bewitched with a telepathic bond of some sort.

Before the situation escalates further, I intervene.

"Let us all take a deep breath."

Crazyjones takes it literally. He closes his eyes and takes a deep breath. Tenderloin and I don't, since we're both dead.

As soon as Crazyjones closes his eyes, Tenderloin runs off, with no more sound than a light breeze rustling the leaves. His bulky size disappears in the blink of an eye.

When Crazyjones opens his eyes after his long deep breath, he looks bewildered, mostly because he still has Juicycrunch raised above his head. Then he shakes his head like he has just awakened from a dream and lowers Juicycrunch the Hoe, which is probably not a hoe at all.

"Where were we?" Crazyjones asks, but then he remembers. "Yes, we are off to dig up the bone Tenderloin found. Wonder where he is now? I haven't seen him all day."

He speaks as if Tenderloin wasn't here recently, which confirms my suspicions. He must be bewitched and bonded. And Tenderloin is probably not the source of the bewitchment, he is just an effect of it.

Crazyjones continues along the track in the forest as if the monster dog incident never happened and asks me again what I am going to do with the bone Tenderloin dug up from the neighbour's field. He assures me that I can tell him even if it is a secret, because he can keep his mouth shut.

I consider telling him while I put a hand on my sword hilt. He won't be able to tell anyone if I shut his mouth for good, as I am trained to do with bewitched people.

But first I have a bone to pick with him.

Chapter 6

As soon as I reach for my sword, still walking behind him, Crazyjones says: "Why are you so... prepared?"

The hoe that rests on his shoulder looks down on me like an ominous ostrich head. The metal beak sways up and down, as if it's rehearsing to hit my head.

I release the grip on the sword and try not to look at Juicycrunch, but instead smell the aroma of the forest. Smell hits your primal instincts more than sight, and I calm down.

So does Juicycrunch. I can feel that.

"How long have you had your dog?" I ask Crazyjones casually, steering the conversation in a new and more trivial direction. That is the reason why people have dogs, isn't it? To have a conversation piece.

"I found him as a pup in the forest." Crazyjones turns his head halfway towards me, in profile and smiles at old memories. "He looked like a cotton ball back then."

"A black cotton ball?" I ask. I remember Tenderloin as black, but it might have been the darkness in the forest.

"More of a greyish hue."

"Grey is no colour."

"Grey is all colours", says Crazyjones as we leave the darkness of the forest and follow the track over flowering meadows. "Just look at all the greyness around you."

Crazyjones points at all the colourful flowers and my suspicion of bewitchment is reinforced: The bewitched only see in greyscale.

I make an extra check to see if I'm on the right track and pick up a common tormentil.

"So which colour is this flower?"

"Ha, that is easy," Crazyjones says and turns all around to lecture me. "It only has four petals, so it must be a tormentil and therefore yellow."

"Maybe you're right, maybe not," I say in a way I think a flirting girl would say it if they wished to be coupled with their chosen one on a flowery meadow.

"What do you mean by 'maybe not'?"

Crazyjones leans forward as the chosen one and gives me a long stare. Juicycrunch the Hoe is looking in another direction or maybe it is sunbathing its shiny beak now that I appear unthreatening.

"Do you want to smell it?" I ask and play shy at the same time. I wriggle with my body, swaying my hips to and fro and look down at my shoes.

"Yes, I can smell if you like."

I play coy and nod.

He bends forward to smell tormentil, but before he gets down to the flower I give him real torment, by hitting his temple as hard as I can with my flowerfree hand.

I have practised this more than swordplay to be honest, for when it comes to my craft, it is easier to go with stealth and innocence and sudden punches, than swordy showoffs. Swordplay impresses ordinary people, but I hunt the extraordinary.

And since I'm small people assume I can't throw in a good punch.

Crazyjones passes out in an instant and slumps down on the ground like a sack of wheat. He releases Juicycrunch the Hoe and I snatch it straight away and start saying the words to make it dormant.

The hoe turns into a bone.

A big haunted bone.

I finish the words to put it to sleep – the right phrase is to make it dormant but that is so impersonal, I like to think of bones sleeping – and wrap it in my special blanket before it can do more harm. Then I move my attention to poor Crazyjones who is lying down amid the flowers.

Chapter 7

When he wakes up, I help him to a sitting position.

"What happened?" he groans.

"Doesn't matter right now," I say and hold a new flower to his face.

"What colour is this flower?"

Instead he looks up at me, squinting his eyes almost shut as the sun is directly behind me. This is intentional, I feel kind of embarrassed for knocking him out like that. I could have persuaded him to give me his bone if I hadn't rushed things, but Tenderloin had put a feeling of desperation and fear in me.

When I was at school all the teachers called me a rushed person, but I wonder if they actually taught me that.

My mother called me a lazy toddler.

"Who are you?" Crazyjones asks eventually and calls me back to the here and now. He seems to have forgotten everything, but best to double-check.

"Miriam."

"Yes, now I remember...I think."

"And what colour is this flower?" I ask again. I hold the flower under his nose.

He looks at it for a few seconds. "It is red. Like the gash on your wrist."

I retract my arm as if I was burned and he apologises immediately. "Sorry, that was rude of me." He helps himself to his feet with a grunt and a yelp of pain and then looks at me.

"What is it?" I ask and look up at him, when he doesn't stop staring.

"Are you really okay, Miriam? You know, with your wrist? That gash looks new." I can feel his breath and his concern tingling my comfort zone.

"It's old. And I'm okay," I say and politely brush him away. He doesn't get it, only retracts a step or two, looking bewildered in his unbewitched state. I would have felt similarly if I woke up with a hangover in a meadow with a total stranger of the opposite sex hovering over me.

Or you would have jumped on him, wouldn't you, a thought in me says. *You were the kind of rushed romantic type, weren't you?*

I hear a part of me laugh harshly, so I stop dwelling in my head and look outside of it at poor, poor Crazyjones. He grimaces when he touches his temple on the right hand side.

"You are okay," I say to regain his attention.

"Thanks."

"I mean bodily," I say and think *that came out the wrong way.* "In a healthy and recuperating way."

"You're a doctor?"

"Sort of, mostly into mending bones." I stand on my tiptoe to take a closer look, as he is a head taller than me. "The bulge in the temple area will disappear in a day or two."

"It feels like my head has been stomped by a horse."

I take that as a compliment, so I reply in kind. "Do you want me to apply a poultice to it, Crazyjones?"

"Crazyjones? Haven't heard that in a while," he says. "No I'm okay, but do we know each other?"

Betwiched persons tend to forget everything after they get bewitched.

"I came because of the neighbours."

"Has there been a complaint about Tenderloin again? And by the way, you don't look like a bailiff."

"I came here to pick a bone."

"Ah, you are that kind of doctor. I should have known. Good," Crazyjones says and smiles with all of his face. "That means The Vault did get the message I sent."

"You sent it?"

"Yup," and Crazyjones nods to himself, quite satisfied. "I did as you folks requested, went to the pigeon post, wrote a note about the bone I found on one of those small parchments, I wrote I found a leg bone, probably animal, but hey, you better check it out and –"

"And you sent the note with one of our pigeons," I finish for him. I have heard this story more times than I can count. Most people marvel at the pigeon post system and wish that they had such a facility at home, but they never concern themselves with the cumbersome detail of actually catching the returned pigeon – no animal likes dead people like me – deciphering the scrawling on the note and translating it into something texty and intelligible. Not to mention actually bringing the hostile pigeon back to the pigeon post, being peppered by bird poop on the way.

But to Crazyjones I seem to be the stuff of legends.

"You are a real Bone Collector."

"The right term is Bone Assembler," I say curtly, but I feel a warm swelling in my chest when I meet his eyes which are wide with admiration.

"Miriam the Bone Assembler," he says like he is tasting fine wine.

I blush, but since I'm dead I'm probably not doing that literally. I'm only remembering the feeling from when I was alive, and right now I'm happy about that.

Crazyjones looks around, his eyes searching without finding anything, before giving me a desperate look.

"I don't know where the bone is."

"I have the bone."

"But I haven't even shown it to you yet!"

"You did show it to me," I say.

"I don't remember."

"The bone bewitched you. This is why you don't remember. That is normal."

"Wow," he says as he digests what I just said. "So it was no animal's leg bone, but a real naughty bone?"

"If that is your term for haunted, you are correct."

"It must have belonged to a big man."

"Indeed," I say and unwrap the bone for him to see and for me to study.

"That's the one!" he says and leans forward.

"Don't touch it," I warn him.

Crazyjones keeps his distance but he has keen eyes. "Why is it engulfed in some sort of bluish flame?"

"We call it soul fire. There must be more bones nearby." I wrap the bone in the blanket again, and lash a rope around it to make sure it won't slip out.

"If that bone is a calf bone he must have been at least twice my size."

"It is not a calf bone."

"An arm bone then?"

"No. Fingerbone."

Chapter 8

"Wow! Fingerbone! That bone must have belonged to a giant!"

"Please keep your voice down," I say as we walk through the meadow.

"There is no one here."

"I like it that way."

"And I like you," Crazyjones says, but turns red when I face him. "I mean, for saving my life and all that."

"Saving your life?"

He nods. "That giant fingerbone would have beaten me to a pulp if you hadn't interfered. I was let off with just a headache, instead of getting my head bashed in."

So untrue, a guilty feeling swirls inside my head, but I ignore it.

"Okay," is the only thing I say in reply.

"Okay? You saved my life!" Suddenly he kneels like a knight before me. "I'm forever in your debt."

"Not mine."

"But without your help I would have been dead and gone!"

"Comes with the job as a bone assembler. Get up now, we don't have time to kneel all day."

I start walking and he gets up to run after me, pestering me with compliments and whatnots. I try to block him out with polite and short answers.

"I would have loved to have a job as a bone assembler," he says.

"No."

"Yes I would. It must be tough getting in."

"Hmpf."

"I would die to get a job like that."

"Yes."

"Can you write me a recommendation?"

"No."

"Please. If I could get in, I would gladly do it for free."

"I do it for free."

"Really?" He runs in front of me to get eye contact. "You mean it, don't you? You must be as kind as you are tough."
"On the contrary."
"So why the free part?"
"Repentance."
"Oh."
"And it is not so fun spending money when you're dead anyway. It keeps reminding you that you are not among the living anymore."
"But you look... alive."
"I'm not."
"If you don't mind me saying, you're too cute to be dead."
Oh, he is also a romantic type, a thought of mine says sarcastically. *Why not unwrap yourself and give him a good long look?*
No.
You should give the meadow a try. Maybe you can get another bone from between his –
"Stop pestering me!" I yell more to myself than to him.
"Sorry," Crazyjones says, and backs away. "But I mean it. Cute in a shy way. I didn't mean to anger you."
"I'm just trying to think and it's hard with you butterflying around me."
He smiles and laughs.
"What is so funny?"
"Butterflies. Tenderloin is shit scared of them. The minute he sees one he runs under a chair to hide. Once I found him in a puddle with just his nose sticking out. Which is why I have painted butterflies on the door to the pantry and on the cookie jars."
"Hm. We can work that to our advantage."
Crazyjones doesn't understand.
"Your dog is bewitched."
"No. Why would he be?"
"Because he has been collecting bones. There are more of them you know," I say and give my wrapped up bone a nod. "You don't make a giant out of one fingerbone."

"He is too small to collect giant fingerbones."

"Wait till you see him now."

"What has happened to him?"

"He killed your neighbour's plow horse."

"Haha," is his reply, but when he sees I'm dead serious, he covers his mouth with his hand.

"How big?"

"As big as the plow horse, with emberglowing eyes and fangs instead of teeth."

"He is a monster?"

"Sort of. And somehow you two and the fingerbone are connected," I say. "To break the spell on your dog, I could kill you…"

"You are joking, right?" Crazyjones looks at the hand on my sword hilt and backs away a few feet, not so sure of the joke.

"We have a saying: Don't kill the messenger," I say with a grin.

"You have a strange sense of humour," he replies and smiles back. "I like it. So if you don't kill me, what do we do?"

"We could find the other fingerbones that Tenderloin has dug up and make them dormant like this one."

"Are you sure that the bone on your back is dormant? I can see the flickering bluish light it emits through the blanket."

Interesting.

"It is probably because you are still connected to it. You are all bonded together, in a necklacey way. I have to break the weakest link."

"So you didn't joke about killing me?"

"Part of the job description is to be hard to read, especially when it comes to people being bound to bones. You might not be under the bone's spell any more, but you do have an affinity to bones, otherwise you wouldn't have seen its soul fire."

"Well, joking or not, please don't kill me," he says half seriously and then turns more serious when it comes to his dog. "And please don't kill Tenderloin either. He is the only one I have."

"You don't make my job easy."

"I can help you."
"Doubt that."
"I'll do anything you say."
Anything?
I like that thought.
"So let's do this together," I hear myself say. "I have a plan."

Chapter 9

An hour later Crazyjones returns with several cookie jars, huffing and puffing and trying to keep his balance, because the jars block his view, making him look like a golem built out of cookie jars. The one blocking his real face has a big red butterfly painted on it, wings outspread and magnified details. The pattern on the wings almost makes it look like a face of some sort, one with dark menacing eyes.

"You are a good painter."

"The devil is in the details," Crazyjones replies and turns sideways so I can see his face. "Where do you want me to place them, Mirry?"

Mirry?

I don't correct him. There is something about the nickname that I like.

Or maybe it is how he says it, another more sinister thought suggests. *Mirry, mirry on the wall...*

I shake off the thought and say, "Just put them down for now. We will figure out the best spot."

He does as he is told and then scratches his head as farmers are wont to do. I guess it comes with the trade, an instinctive action when assessing fields.

And he is definitely assessing now.

We are standing on top of a small hillock halfway between the neighbour's field – Crazyjones gives it an envious look – and a small, but navigable river that flows through the forest. The sandy embankments on the side of the river is ideal for bone digging and a dog loo haven, with unlimited amounts of sand to paw over poop.

"So what is the plan, Mirry?" Crazyjones asks as if we are an established team and in this together. He hands me a cookie from the cookie jar. Obviously he must be a good cook too, the cookie is perfectly round and delicious-looking with zigzags of white and brown chocolate rivers on top.

"Don't waste it on me," I say.

"I want you to have it."

"I'm dead, remember."

"And you will also remember cookies if you taste one, Mirry." He nudges me with an elbow and waves the cookie under my nose.

"Just one then." As I am munching it, I am flooded with sweet, sweet cookie memories, so much so that I slump down on my buttocks with a thump, almost like I'm Inebriated, with a drunken stupid smile.

"Are you okay?" I hear someone say from faraway, but there are too many cookies flying around to see who it is.

I shake my head violently and the memories dissipate. A hand is outstretched in front of me, and I take it. Crazyjones brings me back on my feet.

"What's wrong, Mirry?"

"That was too good", I say while I try to find my balance. "And please don't call me Mirry."

"As you wish, Miss Bone Assembler," Crazyjones says and bows his head. "I'm sorry if I caused you distress."

"Just call me Miriam."

"Miriam."

It's the way he says it, sweet as chocolate, like he is tasting me.

"Yes?" I say, when I see that he is staring at me, expecting something.

"What is the plan?"

"The plan?"

"How to get hold of the rest of the giant fingerbones and pastyfy Tenderloin."

"Not pastyfy. Pacify."

"Means not harming him, right?" Crazyjones gives me a pleading stare.

"Means trying not to harm him."

I haven't had the heart to tell Crazyjones that Tenderloin is probably as dead as I am. As soon as I break the bond, the dog will shrink and die unless I do something stupid.

I'm not going to do something stupid.

Then I remember that's always exactly what I think before I do something stupid.

Crazyjones is eyeing me with a hint of a smile.

"What is it?" I ask.

"The plan, Miriam. I'm still waiting to hear it."

"Oh, the plan?" I say and scratch my head in a farmerly way – *Wait! I would never do that* – but stop midway and end up stroking my chin just like the Vault Master does instead. "The plan is quite simple. We hide the cookie jars behind the rug – you remembered to bring one, right?"

"I brought a sheet instead," he says and pulls a white sheet up from one of the cookie jars. For a moment he reminds me of a magician pulling a white rabbit from his hat.

"That will work," I say.

Crazyjones starts placing the cookie jars on a flat tree stump and puts them three abreast and three atop.

"Put the one with the red butterfly in the middle."

He does as he is told. "And the rest of the plan?"

"I stand in front of the sheeted cookie jars, pretending to break the giant fingerbone. Doing so will alert the others."

"You mean the other bones?"

"Yup. And they will send Tenderloin galloping up here."

"You speak of him as if he was a horse."

"Wait till you see him."

Crazyjones scratches his head. "I just wonder how he could grow so fast. How much time has passed since you got my message?"

"A few days, less than half a week."

"So I have been bewitched for just two or three days? And in that time Tenderloin has grown horsebig and killed the neighbour's plough horse?"

"You told me you borrowed your neighbour's horse for ploughing."

"We are way past ploughing time. When I look at his fields down there, it looks like it has been growing for weeks. Unless he is using magic manure or something on his yield."

"Are you checking up on the neighbour's field?"

"Just comparing, that's all," he says and shrugs, but I feel he is kind of envious of the neighbour's predicted harvest. "And you are evading my question, Miriam. I want to know how long I have been... Crazyjones the Bewitched."

"Hm, let me see," I say to win some time to think. "Do you remember the hole in the roof in your house?"

"Of course, I just saw it. Do you have something to do with it or was it just a visiting meteorite without manners?"

"Neither. You made that hole."

"I would never do that!"

"Yet you did, you said it was to get easy access to light and water."

"I'm not that lazy," he says in his defence. "And when did I do that?"

"You said a month ago."

"Then you must have a serious lag in your pigeon posting system."

"You tell me. I guess it was an old pigeon. They tend to take detours. Or the message might have arrived on foot."

"The pigeon walked?"

"No, the one who ate it for dinner. It is hard to see the difference between a game pigeon and a tame one."

"You punish pigeon poachers, don't you?"

"No, we stopped doing that."

"Why?"

"Because the Vault Master prefers delayed messages instead of not receiving them at all. The threat of punishment makes it far less likely for waylaid messages to get back on track. We even pay a small fee to cover travelling expenses."

"Makes sense." Crazyjones looks at me and returns to the previous conversation. "And then what happens after you pretend to break the giant fingerbone in front of Tenderloin?"

"Tenderloin will try to assault me, but then you – you are hidden behind the stack of cookie jars by the way – you unsheet the butterflied cookie jars. They will give Tenderloin a scare, and I will entangle him with my rope if I can or follow him to his lair where I'm sure he keeps the rest of the bones."

"Almost sounds too easy."

"Simple is best," I say.

But an hour later as I'm pretending to chop the bone in two with my sword, it doesn't sound easy at all.

And it happens way too fast.

The roar that engulfs the forest, the loud thumping up the hill and the fangish growl and angered ember eyes, brings back memories of being scared.

"Don't you dare!" rumbles the big hulking figure and rises on its hind legs in front of me.

I lose my composure.

The next thing I hear is the sword clanking on the ground beside me and I'm swaying as my legs are actually shaking from memories of fear.

But then the table turns when Crazyjones unsheets the cookie jars, and I botch the plan by acting simply stupid.

Chapter 10

Tenderloin's majestic roar turns into a squeak when he sees all the nine butterflies at once. He remembers being scared all too well, and when he turns around to run, I can almost imagine what he must have looked like when he was an ordinary dog.

I act without thinking, throwing the lasso and ensnaring him, never having time to think that this was a stupid action – me being so small compared to him – before I'm mopping the undergrowth with my body as we race through the forest. At least I managed to pick up my sword, and I clutch it with all my might.

"Mirry!" I hear from somewhere behind me. "Let go of the rope!"

I wish I could, but I have been entangled as well. Next time I throw a lasso, I will remember not to stand in the coil of rope.

If there is going to be a next time.

Tenderloin runs as if possessed – which, of course, he is – but now more with fear than haunted bone, intermittently whimpering, now and then throwing a glance backwards to look for the terrifying butterflies. My presence seems to frighten him even more, maybe because both of my arms have somehow gotten wrapped up in the sheet, and I'm flailing them around in a panic, making me look like a gigantic white butterfly bumping along the forest floor.

"Mirry, Mirry!" Crazyjones' yells get fainter and fainter.

"I'm here!" I yell back as best as I can, and the next moment I'm out of the forest, hitting the sandy embankment and sledging along the river on my buttocks. I manage to halfway sit up, trying frantically to loosen the rope with my sword free hand. But it is impossible, the rope has dug into the flesh of my thighs and the flapping sheet is not making things easier.

In this instance I'm glad I'm undead and not able to feel pain very well. Instead of memories of pain, I get memories of tobogganing in winter, and feel a misplaced joy to the point of wanting more when we suddenly stop.

I can see why the race is over.

We have arrived at the riverbank.

The sand here has been dug in.

Tenderloin shakes off the scare and grows bigger and threatening now that he is close to the other bones.

Even I can feel them in my bones, pun intended, even as I'm still enveloped by my happy memories of tobogganing. But they evaporate when Tenderloin opens his jaws filled with white and all too pointy fangs.

"I will kill you!" he roars and stomps the ground like an angry ox.

"Sure you are not going to eat me first?" I yell back to buy some time. "That is way meaner than to kill me and then eat me."

He stops for one second to think. "I never said I was hungry, did I?"

Meanwhile I untangle myself from the rope and the sheet, and get up on my feet, ready to fight, going into the stance called 'The Old Swordsman and the Beast.'

Somewhere behind me I hear Crazyjones yelling my name.

In front of me, Tenderloin narrows his red eyes and grins fangily.

"I have a sharp toothpick," I warn him.

"No, you brought the bone," he says and licks his mouth.

Only now do I understand why the sword hilt feels awkward. I'm not wielding the sword, my hands are clutching the giant fingerbone. It emits a clear bluish flame, confirming my suspicion that it's close to the other bones.

"I'll break it!" I threaten and grab the bone with both hands, ready to smash it over my knee.

"You are only going to hurt yourself, little bug," Tenderloin laughs. "It's too thick for you."

"I'm a Bone Assembler", I say as calmly as I can. "I know how to break bones. In fact, it is my specialty, breaking things."

Especially rules.

"Don't you dare, little one," the beast roars. "If you break my precious thumb bone, I'll break your back. And then I'm going to make you wince and wriggle with pain like a little worm on a hook."

The beast takes a step forward, but then suddenly stops, as we both hear nearby yelling from behind a stretch of reeds.

"Mirry! Mirry! Hold out! I'm coming to the rescue!"

"Crazyjones has a soft spot for you," Tenderloin says. "Let's strike a deal. I'll let you have him, if you give me the bone." Tenderloin is on his hind legs, towering over me and stretching out his front paw as a hand. "Don't be foolish, give me the bone and then leave."

I shake my head.

"So you want to die? I can throw that in the bargain as well. You and him corpsing on the riverbank."

"Step away from her, Tenderloin!" Crazyjones says, approaching from the reeds with my sword in hand. He glances quickly at me. "Get behind me, Mirry!"

I backstep with my eyes still locked on Tenderloin. He growls and follows me slowly, but then Crazyjones jumps in between us, brandishing my sword.

Tenderloin roars with anger. "I'll kill you, manling!"

Crazyjones replies with equal anger: "Don't be rude to the one that spoon fed you and saved your life!"

"That dog you talk of is no more," the beast says. "He died chewing the bone. And I woke up."

"You'll do as I say, or.. or…" Crazyjones hesitates. I can see that he is no sword fighter, unless there is a stance called 'Stupid Farmer Unintentionally Baits Himself'.

"Give me the sword!" I say and try to grab it from him.

But he is stubborn and refuses to release it. "No, get behind me, Mirry!"

Or maybe he thinks he is being chivalrous.

It doesn't matter.

Tenderloin grabs his chance and leaps at us.

It all happens so fast, but luckily I have been trained for such situations. I kick Crazyjones in the shin to get him to release his grip and snatch the sword but Tenderloin rams into me before I can stab him. I'm hurled into the sand, but I manage a controlled landing and dodge sideways and avoid Tenderloin's second ramming, but he snaps at me in passing so I lose the bone from my other hand.

It lands in the sand, looking like the last dying log in a campfire, sputtering bluish flames.

Tenderloin loses interest in me. Fast as lightning the huge black and spiky body lunges for the bone.

No!

I'm too far away. But someone else is reaching for the bone, getting between it and the massive beast.

No, no, no!

Crazyjones throws himself at the bone right before Tenderloin approaches with massive jaws that snap shut the next instant.

I hear a sickening crunch that is followed by a shriek.

Chapter 11

I don't know which one of us who made the shriek.
It might have been me.

The next moment, Crazyjones goes limp and is thrown like a ragdoll up in the air, spraying the surrounding area red. He hits the sand with a heavy thump and a caved in chest, his eyes staring at nothing.

The giant fingerbone makes a lot of somersaults before hitting the ground with the pointy end of the finger, digging itself into the sand, standing perpendicular up from the ground.

Tenderloin gives the bone a hungry look, before his ember eyes close shut and he emits a devastating howl of pain. Then he starts trashing and bashing and shrinking rapidly.

What is happening?

Then I understand. Crazyjones must have been killed instantly when Tenderloin crushed his chest. The beast broke the bond when he killed Crazyjones. And when the bond broke, the bewitchment of the poor dog Tenderloin ceased in an uncontrolled fashion.

The pent-up energy evaporates from Tenderloin in bursts of soul fire from eyes, ears, mouth and also the hind parts. He looks like he is being barbecued from the inside. Then he starts swelling like a balloon.

He is going to burst.

That would be bad, very bad with so many haunted bones lying around.

Without thinking I run to the now dog-sized monster and incantate a spell to save him and then let the excess energy run through my body. My arms and legs flail wildly, but I don't die, since I'm already dead and trained to be a lightning conductor for soul fire.

Memories of pain flash past in a whirl.

Then I get a warm sensation of something wet stroking my hand.

I look down at a creature that is part dog and part beast licking my hand. He is not much bigger than a cookie jar. Actually he looks a bit like a cookie jar, minus the painted butterfly, plus stubby legs, a short tail and a head sticking out of it. And some kind of fur that reminds me of a hedgehog.

"Shouldn't you be dead?"

"Woof?"

"Well, it's a good sign that you are barking and not talking," I say and stand up and look at the dog. I stroke his fur and focus on his body.

Of course!

The rabbit foot I gave him as a snack. A lucky charm has saved his life, or at least bought the little dogbeast a respite from death.

I wonder how much of the beast is still in him.

"Can you stand on your hind legs, Tenderloin?"

"Woof!"

Tenderloin the dog actually tries, but stops when he understands there are no rewarding goodies. Then he runs barking over to Crazyjones and licks his face.

No reaction.

Crazyjones is stone dead.

Tenderloin whimpers and gives me a sad doggy stare.

I wipe something from my eyes. At first I think it is blood or river water, but when I taste it, it brings back memories of the big salty ocean and my longing for the horizon when the bullying got too tough.

One day I will get to the other side, says the thought from that day when I felt all alone in the world and I dreamed of being someone else.

I kneel in front of Crazyjones.

"I will not leave you here alone," I say. Then I close his eyes and say some words that I'm not supposed to say.

When I leave one hour later on a raft of roped fingerbones – a good thing that haunted bones float on water – I'm travelling with a yapping dog and a wrapped up corpse.

And some very, very stupid ideas that will get me into more problems when I return to The Vault.

Still, I'm smiling. And I imagine that Crazyjones is doing the same under the sheet.

Interlude: A lesson in world building
Chapter 12

"Today we are going to have a lesson on how the world is put together," the old rattler announces.

Maybe he isn't that old, Jim Wise surmises, but for the other kids - a baker's dozen today – he is just as ancient as the vacated and overgrown shrine they have their classes in, next to the crossroads between Hunker Street and Wicker Alley, not far from the city gates – you can see the turrets through the holes in the roof – and right by the riverside.

The old rattler reminds Jim Wise of a priest with that ragged robe he is dressed in, and he rattles like a ghost when he moves about with all the cylindrical scroll containers which he has strapped to his body.

Maybe he is a ghost on a light penance, Jim Wise thinks, *so he got to drag scrolls around instead of a ball and chain.*

The old rattler stands behind a plinth, treating it as if it were a desk – the statue which had been on top is long gone – and looks over his class of scruffy kids that sit in a semicircle on the floor.

Jim's friend Capsize – his father was a captain lost at sea, hence the nickname (even if Capsize insists he got it because he wears a cap) – raises his arm.

"Yes, Capsize. You have a question about the world?"

"You said 'put together'," Capsize says and frowns. "Are you talking of... coupling?"

"No," the old rattler answers, eyeing Capsize to see if the brat is pulling his leg.

But Capsize keeps his not-too-smart face straight. For him it is a valid question.

Capsize's mother used to be in the coupling trade, but she got too smart for it and now she has other people to couple for her, while she tells them how to do it pennywise and with their teeth intact.

Which is more than you can say about the old rattler. He has lost half of his teeth and he is only paid in small change and leftover edibles. He keeps the small change in his pockets and the breadcrumbs in his grizzled beard after he has eaten his fill of dried bread.

The old rattler walks down from the platform the plinth is on, squats down in front of the class and rolls out an old musty map that he anchors with some lead weights in each corner.

"This is a map of the known world," the old rattler says.

"Geography is boring," Capsize announces after a quick scan of the weatherworn and worm-eaten map.

"And who are you to say that?" the old rattler asks.

"Because I am a boarlock from Tuskany!" Capsize says and sticks his split carrot – his mother forces him to eat one every day to keep a healthy tan – down between his lower lip and gums to act as tusks.

"I bet a copper coin that those tusks will fall out before the class is over," the old rattler says unaffected by the tusky display and looks directly at Capsize. "You in?"

Capsize just nods. He can't speak with his carrot tusks without losing the wager.

The old rattler looks down at the map again and says: "We can start with boarlocks and Tuskany."

"Do they really exist?" a wide eyed young girl says. Her name is Vinni and Jim Wise really likes her. "Or does Capsize say so only to bump my goose?" she asks, looking at her goosebumps on her forearm.

"Neither boarlocks nor Tuskany exists," the old rattler replies, "unless you swap the first letter in each word with another one. Let me show you." The old rattler writes "boarlock" with a piece of chalk on the plinth, then crosses over the "bo" and writes a "w" above it.

"Warlocks," wide eyed Vinni says, goosebumping for real. "They are dangerous and live with the witches up north."

"Correct. Warlocks and witches live in the Peccaran Lands with the rest of the barbarians, unless they have a good reason to hide under the bed or in the closet of bad-behaving children."

Jim Wise raises his hand.

"Yes, Jim Wise." The old rattler smiles. "Do you have a warlock in your closet?"

Jim Wise shakes his head. "No, but I heard the warlocks and witches also roam in the Northern Territories." He points at the big swathe of land right below the Peccaran snow-covered north.

The old rattler nods. "The Northern Territories are disputed between us and the Peccarans and have been for a long time. So it is only natural that warlocks and witches follow in the wake of the Peccaran incursions, just as our nobles follow in the wake of our incursions." He then picks up the piece of chalk and says: "Let's return to Capsize's Tuskany."

When the old rattler writes "Tuskany" on the plinth, crosses over the "T" and writes a "H" above it, Jim Wise peeks at his silent carrot-tusked friend who dries off dribble on his sleeve when he thinks no one is looking.

All to win the wager and a lousy coin, Jim Wise thinks and then he looks down at the map and raises his hand.

"Yes, Jim?"

"Tuskany is Huskany. The empty land in the south, between us and Dunvis."

"Dunvis or the Far South as people here in the city call it," the old rattler says and points at the peninsula at the bottom of the map. "But Dunvis used to go all the way up here, all through Huskany."

The old rattler lets his index finger traverse from the southernmost tip northwards through the peninsula, through the empty land of Huskany and all the way up an image of a big city.

"No one owns Huskany," one of the more well dressed kids says, who has been picking his nose up to this point. "My father says it is lawless land and you can't trade through it, but have to sail around."

"Your trading father is right, Nom," the old rattler says. "But Huskany used to be a land of plenty and Dunvis used to have its capital right here." He keeps his finger pointed at the city.

"That is our capital!" wide eyed Vinni says, even more wide-eyed than usual.

Jim Wise makes a light cough.

The old rattler gives Jim Wise a sideway glance and nods. "Enlighten us."

"The city was called Vastrual when the Far South was in command, but then King Grimber took it by force and renamed it after himself, but most people don't use that name anymore, now that we are at loss for kings and queens and so we just call it City or Capital."

"Couldn't have said it better myself," the old rattler says. "So who rules today instead of the queens and kings, Jim?"

"The city council. Consisting of the most powerful families."

"And?"

"And the Vault Master from The Vault," Jim Wise says with some hesitation, adding a discreet sign to ward off evil.

His father has said it brings bad luck to speak of the dead, especially the walking ones.

"How do you know all those things?" Vinni blurts out after shifting her gaze between Jim and the map plenty of times. "You read the map like a book."

"My father has the same map on the wall in the main hall."

"Is he a noble?" well dressed Nom asks with an index finger still dug up his nose.

"He is an innkeeper. And when I serve the guests I stay around the tables enough to pick up conversations."

"That makes Jim Wise sophisticated," the old rattler explains.

"What is soffis-ti-cated?" Vinni asks with a frown that makes her eyes almost look normal-sized.

"It is–"

"Look!" Capsize yells out and immediately loses the wager and both his carrot tusks as he runs to a man-sized hole in the wall on the riverside of the shrine, too enthralled by what he sees to bother about the wager anymore.

He points at a small figure who is steering a craft made of big bones.

"It looks like a big skeleton hand!" wide-eyed Vinni informs everyone as they all jostle around the hole which is way too small for the whole class.

"It is a big skeleton hand," the old rattler informs in a grave voice, looking over their heads. "She is steering them old bones. Haunted bones."

The small figure steering, a dark bob-haired girl with a sword at her side, looks more concentrated to keep her course in the currents than afraid of standing in the palm of the skeletal hand that looks like it could squash her like a bug.

That girl must be one of the undead, Jim Wise thinks and he looks at the swathed corpse that lies at her feet. *Wonder if that poor fellow is on his way to become one.*

When the undead girl discovers that she is being watched, she smiles like a living one and waves her hand at the thronged hole in the shrine.

They wave – or ward off evil – back, so Capsize, who's in front, is pushed out of the hole. He is about to fall in the river and make a grim reality of his name – he cannot swim – when the cute undead girl says some sing-songy words.

The next moment Capsize is flung back into the hole like he was a catapulted stone, scattering his classmates like dry beans. His trajectory thumps him hard on the map, in the big chunk of sea where his father took a deep dive, and where he squeals like a stung pig.

"Was that magic?" Vinni says and her eyes almost pop out of her face.

"It must be," Jim Wise says matter-of-factly and he acts like his father whenever the undead show up and do their tricking stuff: Talk it down.

"How can you tell?" Vinni wants to know.

"That is easy," Jim says and points at Capsize. "Capsize never loses a wager. And he never cries either. So he must be affected by magic."

Capsize who is sleeving his eyes is quick to nod in agreement and for the rest of the lesson he is cursing the magic that makes his eyes water and also forces him to stand while they continue traversing the map with the old rattler's finger.

Part 2: Vaulting with Crazyjones
Chapter 13

He wakes with a jolt and sits upright in his bed.

Tenderloin yaps and scrambles for him, but his paws are waddling in the air. Unknown hands hold the dog in midair, then slowly hand him the dog.

Tenderloin is in ecstasy, as if all butterflies have been wiped from the earth and the rest of his existence will be carefree, only seeking the pleasure of pooping at the neighbour's doorstep, eating food that is meant for someone else and digging for bones.

Bones, he thinks. *I remember something about bones.*

While petting Tenderloin he looks around in the semi-darkness.

This is not home. At least not as I remember it.

He looks up as if hoping to see a hole in the roof – he has no idea why – but there isn't one, only more darkness.

"Good mourning."

Then he remembers the fact that someone held his dog a moment ago. The hands belong to a female person, he can see that, but she is not recognizable. She is sitting at his bedside, in a very non-intrusive manner. Almost like a piece of furniture.

"Good morning," he replies eventually.

She looks at him as if he is being funny. Tenderloin jumps off of the bed to chase something interesting in the dark reaches of the room, and as the dog sniffs around in the darkness, Crazyjones can see a couple of red eyes peering out of the shadows close to where his pet would be.

That is not normal, not normal at all.

"Come back here, Tenderloin!" he commands.

Tenderloin returns as he is told, along with the red eyes. They actually sit in his head where his doggy eyes used to be. Not sad and pleading, but emberglowing.

"What has happened to you?" he says and pets the dog.

There is something wrong with his fur also.

It is spiky, almost needle-like.

"He ate a lucky charm," the woman replies. "A rabbit foot. That kept him in between."

"In between what?"

"Between life and death. I have registered him as unliving with the name Tenderloin Redeye. I added the last part so he does not accidentally end up on the dinner table."

"Am I in an infirmary?"

"No," the woman replies. He can see that her skin has a greenish tinge. She wipes away some dribble from the corner of her mouth with her sleeve and reaches out a hand, but he hesitates to shake it.

"In a pest house?"

"No."

"Are you sick?"

"No."

He gingerly takes her hand.

It is stone cold.

Or maybe I am having a fever.

"Selina Sekunda," is the woman's introduction.

"John Kraze."

She lifts an eyebrow.

"Strange. You are registered as Crazyjones."

"I have been called that. But it's just a nickname really."

"Do you want me to change it? I'm sure Miss Huckerpucker wouldn't mind."

"Who is Miss Huckerpucker?"

"The one that turned you in." She gives him a long look. "You don't remember, do you?"

"No."

"Try to think," Selina Sekunda says and leans forward. "Do you recall someone from the last few days, a young woman of short stature and with a face that some men would call cute?"

His memories are a mumbled mess, that is for sure. Almost like someone has turned him inside out and then stuffed everything back in without any order to it.

Then Crazyjones catches a glimmer of something.

"I think there was something about a mirror. Did I see someone in a mirror perhaps?"

"Not bad," Selina Sekunda says and leans back. "Not a mirror, but Miriam. Miriam Huckerpucker. The one who brought you in."

As soon as Selina Sekunda says that, he is flooded with memories. Big bad monsterdogs, dying plow horses, butterflies and cookies run amok in his head and he falls back in his bed gasping, trying to catch some air.

"I can't breathe."

"You can if you want to," Selina Sekunda points out. "Just try to relax".

When he doesn't, she strokes his arm and says some words which soothe him and the panic evaporates along with the cookied-butterfly-monsterdog galloping like a horse through his head.

He is breathing heavily.

Selina Sekunda gives him an ironic stare through a face otherwise dead of expression.

"You find me funny."

"Miriam found you funny as well."

He definitely remembers someone with that name, someone he met recently, cute as hell and who made him smile. The remembrance is accompanied by an elevated heartbeat.

"Where is Miriam?"

"Upstairs."

"And where am I?"

"You are in the mortuary, reviving." Selina Sekunda pauses for a moment to let it sink in. "And yes, you are dead."

Utter silence for a few seconds.

Then Crazyjones lets out a scream that scares Tenderloin into the darkness, and makes Selina Sekunda put a hand on his forehead, incantating words that sends him to sleep, or at least to the memory of sleeping.

Chapter 14

When Crazyjones awakes again, he says the first thing that comes to his mind.

"I'm dead." The instant Crazyjones says the words, his mind sends a shockwave of jumbled memories through him and his body starts to quiver violently.

This time Selina Sekunda doesn't lay a hand on him but says calmly, "Focus on your breathing."

"But I'm dead!" he screams and scares Tenderloin off of the bed for the second time.

Selina Sekunda is unaffected by his tantrum.

"Remembering life helps, Crazyjones." She puts a hand on him and looks into his eyes. "Breathing is life. So breathe."

He tries.

Breathe in, breathe out, breathe in, breathe out...

And it actually calms him.

"But I'm still dead, ain't I?" he asks in between the breaths.

"I prefer the term unliving, simply because it reminds me of life." She releases her grip and ruminates on the thought. "It is almost like unthinking."

"Unthinking?" he asks.

"Makes you think, doesn't it?"

"You are quite a philosopher," he says ironically, not feeling comfortable or casual being a revived corpse in a mortuary.

She takes it as a compliment. "I have plenty of time to think while reviving people."

"So you woke me to... unlife."

"No. Miss Huckerpucker did."

"Why not say Miriam?"

"My job is to get you to think", she says with a sly undertone.

Okay, maybe she wasn't a philosopher in real life, her thievish tone doesn't match that profession.

"So what has happened to me?"

"Miriam woke you to unlife, but I have to do the actual revival. She never had the patience for that, always running off on new adventures."

Crazyjones sits up in his bed. "She hasn't left, has she?"

"No. She is grounded due to that show she put on." Selina Sekunda steeples her fingers while judging Miss Miriam Huckerpucker's performance. "Rafting in on a giant skeleton hand was unorthodox at best, but she was set on getting you on the fastest track to the mortuary. It did raise a hue and cry and got the City Council breathing down our necks."

"Is that a problem?"

"They barely tolerate us."

"Us? And who are we exactly?"

"Ah, of course, you don't remember. I forgot that." Selina Sekunda pats his hand in a reassuring way. "You are in The Vault."

Crazyjones thinks for a second, visiting old memories of bringing his surplus food to the city market. "The Vault. You mean the big bad dome that looks like it crash landed in the middle of the capital?"

"Not a bad description," she says and pats him again. "There might still be hope for you."

"So when can I see Miriam? I need some answers."

Crazyjones tries to get out of bed, but Selina Sekunda tucks him back in. It is not actually a real bed, but a stone slab with a mattress on. There are more of those around, but they are both devoid of mattresses and patients.

"Relax, Crazyjones. You will see her in time. And she is not leaving anytime soon. As I said, she has been grounded by the Vault Master."

"She could run away."

"True. She has done that before, so the Vault Master put a spell on her before he left to meet the City Council." Selina Sekunda shakes her head and sighs. "Between you and me, Miss Huckerpucker is rash and not good at long term planning. Don't ever tell her that, unless you want her to be rash. And when she is rash she does things we all regret, and some might call stupid. Flatface even called her that once, face to face."

"What happened?"

"She was rash, then got grounded, then ran away, got caught, and was grounded again."

"Poor Miriam."

"Oh, don't feel sorry for her. She loves being grounded, but pretends not to."

"Why?"

"She likes to read novels, especially the romantic and sentimental ones." Selina Sekunda looks slantwise at him. "You don't have to tell her that I said that."

"I won't."

"Sure?"

"I promise."

They shake hands on it and then she throws in some more gossip about Miriam.

"She is too memorised for my taste. It is almost like she is still alive. It must be all the reading that's done it. I just stick to my own memories, not inventing new ones on the fly."

"Well, if I can't see her, and not even be allowed out of bed, what am I supposed to do?"

"You can read," Selina Sekunda suggests and retrieves a book from under the stone slab. "Miriam gave me this to give to you. It is the first book in the Earthy Soft Rose trilogy."

"Is it good?"

"Not at all."

Crazyjones takes it. "Have you even read it?"

"No. And I never will. It's pulp fiction. The cover says it all."

Crazyjones looks at the cover. It is glaring with colours and portrays a half-dressed couple in a dramatic embrace, surrounded by what looks like animated rose bushes.

"It looks pulpy," he says, agreeing with Selina on that account.

"Indeed. But Miriam asked you to treat it with care since there is a written dedication on the inside of the cover. She also said you could start there."

"And when I am finished reading the book? What then?"

"The Vault Master will return long before then. City Council meetings last awhile, but not that long," Selina Sekunda says and looks at the thick book Crazyjones is holding.

"The Vault Master wants to talk with me?"

"Most certainly. Everybody has to pass the interview to get the job."

"Which job?"

"A bone assembler in service of The Vault. That's why I'm reviving you. And I'm gonna kill you if you're not doing well."

"You're joking right?"

"No", she says dead serious. "Unlife is only allowed for us Vault dwellers."

Chapter 15

Crazyjones reclines with the book, while Selina Sekunda tends to other duties.

"Yell if you need me," she says before she disappears into the darkness. "There should be enough oil in the lamp if you keep from oversizing the flame."

"I'll keep it as it is."

"Good. Try not to think too much in the meantime."

"Why?"

"It will probably make you panic, and I have done enough babysitting for today," she says with greenish and swollen lips. Black dribble is bubbling in the corner of her mouth.

She must have noticed that he saw the dribble, because she instantly wipes it away with her hand.

"What happened to you, Selina?"

"Ate poison," she says and sticks her tongue out. It looks like a black oversized leech. When it retracts into her mouth, Crazyjones tries not to shiver. "Anything else?" she asks.

"No, thanks."

"I'll leave you to it then," she says and looks at the book in his lap. "Good luck. You'll need it for the Earthy Soft Rose."

"I'll manage," he says and gives her a half-hearted grin.

He is not sure what the grimace she returns is supposed to mean.

Probably an attempt at a smile from contorted face muscles of a poison victim.

She turns to leave.

Who killed her? he wonders.

The next moment she blurs into darkness. Her steps fade away like a whisper, followed by a creaking sound, probably from a door – *or a coffin? I'm in a mortuary after all* – and then there is total silence.

Crazyjones sits closer to the flame.

The book cover looks like trash, but it feels like heaven compared to the bleak surroundings.

Am I really dead?

He quells the impulse to check his pulse, but instead tries to find a cosy position on the mattressed stone slab, close to the flickering oil lamp.

He has never been much of a book reader, but the alternatives are nil, except from getting total panic or passing out.

And if I'm dead I'm probably not able to pass out anyway.

He starts with the dedication, and discovers that authors are no better at dedications than doctors are at writing prescriptions, but eventually he manages to decipher the scribble. He reads it aloud to himself in a low voice.

"If you want this job, remember that it was suicide. You didn't do it for me or to be brave."

It is signed with M.

Miriam!

He realises all of a sudden that this is no dedication – not that he has read any and can compare – but a message from Miriam to him. He remembers faintly that he told her he wanted a job like hers, and he also remembers that he gave her one of his home baked cookies and felt some deep contentment when she said it was all too good.

He looks up from the book and into the flame.

Mirry, what are you trying to tell me between the lines? Do you want me to hang around here with you?

The thought tickles like having butterflies in his stomach, but then he starts to doubt.

Maybe it is just professional. She is recruiting for The Vault. She said I had an affinity with haunted bones, didn't she?

Crazyjones recalls the blue flame the big bad fingerbone was engulfed in.

Was it soul fire she called it?

Not that it matters.

He flicks through the book to look for any more scribbles, but there aren't any, just rows and rows of impersonal text. He had hoped for a scribbled heart, which is stupid and just makes him frustrated.

When Tenderloin returns from wherever he has been, Crazyjones lets him jump up on the stone slab. He starts petting his dog and it would have reminded him of the good old days if it hadn't been for the hedgehog-like fur and the emberglowing eyes that glow faintly in the dark, and that he is sitting in a mortuary, waiting for a job interview where one of the conditions probably is suicide.

In that sense it is a positive that I'm dead already.

Chapter 16

Selina Sekunda comes back after what feels like an eternity.

"The Vault Master has returned. You're next on his plate."

Crazyjones doesn't like the metaphor, but he keeps his mouth shut. He puts on his shoes and rises from the bed.

"The dog will stay here." Selina Sekunda's voice makes it clear that this is not up for debate.

"Take good care of him."

"Don't have to," she says. She bends down to pet the little beast, but instead she utters some words in a strange language, and Tenderloin slumps down like a discarded ragdoll, the light going out of his eyes. "He will be inactive until you return."

"Was what you just said, a spell of some sort?"

"Yes. It is the same I'm going to do to you if you don't pass the interview, but then in a permanent way." She puts a hand on his shoulder and looks him in the eyes. "If I were you, I would be more concerned about the interview than your dog."

Then she turns him around and steers him through the dark mortuary, up some stairs, along a corridor where he can see the starry night outside, through doors and more corridors. From one half-open room he can hear subdued voices, in another room light flickers on the wall which must come from a fireplace. He tries to have a peek, but is pushed on.

"This way, snoopy."

They cross a bridge over a big darkness that echoes their steps and when he looks down he can see faint lights which remind him of reflected starlight in black water. The lights are swaying slightly just like ripples on the water, but the air is too dry for there to be a large body of water down below.

"What is underneath us?" he asks.

"That is the vault with all the keepsakes and ancient writings," Selina Sekunda replies without stopping. "You will get to know it in time."

If I pass the interview, he thinks gloomily.

Crazyjones looks at her, asking: "Do you think I'll pass?"

"Ask me instead what I feel."

"What do you feel then?"

"Very little except nuisance from all your questions. But that is hopefully a memory by tomorrow," she says, looking at him askance.

Crazyjones takes the hint and shuts up.

He is escorted through more stairs and corridors, always going upwards, until they at last stop in front of a well hinged door. It has five hinges, instead of the ordinary two, and Selina Sekunda knocks on this door and someone from the inside says "Come in!"

She opens the door, and shoos him through, before she closes it behind him.

"Welcome," says a small hooded figure from behind a big office table at the other end of the room. He is illuminated by a bluish flame from a candle light except –

– *that is no candle light, but a thin and long bone.*

The bone is tucked in a candlestick, so it is easy to mistake it for an ordinary white candle. And Crazyjones probably would have, were it not for the blue flame and how he had seen the giant fingerbone emit a similar flame.

Soul fire.

"Don't be shy. Come forward," the small figure at the table encourages him. A small hand motions at Crazyjones.

Crazyjones walks cautiously forward.

This is easier said than done, for in the faint blue light, Crazyjones can see that the office must have been ransacked or is in the middle of being refurbished: lots of things lie scattered around in a random fashion. He avoids the nearest chair that is lying on its back with legs sticking out like tripwire, steps over a drawer placed upright as a wall – way better than going near a small table with a house of cards built on top – and keeps zigzagging his way to the chair on his side of the office table. There is a pillow on the chair, with a note stuck with a pin saying "Remove me."

Crazyjones stops for a second and looks at the hooded figure. Of course the face is hidden, but from the shrunken size he suspects the Vault Master must be a very old man. Or a woman.

"Where do you want me to place the pillow?"

"The table will be fine."

Crazyjones puts the pillow on the table and sits down.

"So you are the famous Crazyjones?"

"I wouldn't say so," Crazyjones replies. "I'm just a farmer."

"With quite a reputation after rafting into the city on a big skeletal hand."

"I wasn't aware."

"It doesn't matter. People need something to talk about. Now they have it. And we have plenty of new bones. Miss Huckerpucker told me you notified The Vault when you found the haunted bone. The thumb bone, I believe."

He nods, but when the hooded figure keeps silent, he also says, "Yes."

"We appreciate the gesture."

"Thank you. I understood from Miri– Miss Huckerpucker that you had some delays in your pigeon postal service."

"Nothing that is not fixable," the hooded figure says and leans forward. "You are far worse off, I'm afraid. I heard you were killed during the bone retrieval?"

This is awkward.

"Well, actually…" Crazyjones says, and then he doesn't know what to say. Even if Miriam said he should say he committed suicide, he can't bring himself to lie. It is an important job interview after all.

And if you lie now, it is going to bite your backside sooner or later, he thinks.

"Or was it an accident?" the hooded figure suggests.

"No. It was deliberate."

"That is ambiguous enough to call it a suicide," the hooded figure decides and reaches out a hand. "Congratulations."

"For killing myself?"

"No, for passing the interview," says the small hooded figure, waiting for the handshake.

The total surprise of passing the interview, the whys and hows of it, dissipate when Crazyjones shakes the hand. It is not an old wrinkled hand as he suspected, but a child's hand.

Chapter 17

The small figure unhoods itself. It is indeed a child. The boy can't be more than seven or eight.

Crazyjones gawks at the child who looks back up at him.

No, he is not looking at me. He is looking through me.

Crazyjones looks away, but when he looks back – he can't stop himself from doing it – the child still stares through him.

"Do you mind lighting the oil lamp?" the child says. "I believe the matchbox is next to it."

The child must be blind.

"Of course," Crazyjones replies, but first he waves his hand in front of the child's face. Back and forth, back and forth. The blue light on the tip of the bone flickers slightly.

No reaction.

But then the child says, "I don't need you fanning me."

"Sorry." Crazyjones instantly takes down the hand, flicks a match and lights the oil lamp. A clear orange glow lights up the table and the nearby surroundings.

The child's eyes stop staring through him. Instead they focus on his face.

"So you are the famous Crazyjones," the child says. "I'm Cerrakin, also known as the Vault Master."

"But you are a child."

"Looks can be deceiving", Cerrakin says. "But you saw me in the dark."

"You were close to the candle – I mean the bone."

"Well, I didn't see you," Cerrakin says and then leans to the side to look behind Crazyjones. "Which route did you take?"

Crazyjones turns around. "I went to the right there", he points at the fallen chair, "and then over the standing drawer." He then looks back at Cerrakin the Vault Master. "Was it some kind of test?"

Cerrakin nods and seems very pleased. "Miriam was correct. You have the affinity to see soul fire very well."

"And you didn't see me at all?"

"I barely saw the soul fire itself. You passed the interview before you sat down. To be accurate, it was when you removed the pillow."

"It had a note stuck to it."

"And you managed to read it. Amazing."

"What about the killing-yourself-part of the interview?"

"In your case a formality," Cerrakin says and rises from the chair. "Do you mind helping me tidy up before we continue the conversation? I can get us some tea as well."

Crazyjones nods and over the course of the next minutes, Cerrakin orders him around to place the different furniture at the right spots, while Cerrakin himself takes down the house of cards. Afterwards they sit down for a cup of tea. A servant brings in a tray with a steaming tea kettle and two cups.

"I heard you like to drink your tea warm," says Cerrakin while he pours with both hands on the teapot. "So I fill yours only half full. The tea in the cup loses heat faster that way, but it won't be cold before you empty it."

"You could just refill it with some more hot tea if it got cold," Crazyjones feels emboldened enough to say.

Cerrakin smiles. "So we have got a new thinker in our ranks? Not bad. Not bad at all."

"Do you have many applicants?"

"We call them suiciders." Cerrakin sits down after pouring. "We have a steady stream, but too few pass the job interview. Sugar?"

"Yes, please."

Cerrakin dumps a lump of sugar in Crazyjones' cup and then one in his own.

"Not to be rude," Crazyjones says while he is using a spoon to dissolve the sugar, "but the interview didn't seem too hard."

"You are a special case. And you want the job, don't you?"

"Yes, why?"

"Applicants don't commit suicide to get a job," Cerrakin says while stirring the spoon in the steaming tea. "They commit suicide when

63

they don't get the job."

"True enough."

"The suicide part is a Vault secret. Don't tell anyone outside these walls."

"I won't."

"I suspect someone gave you a hint though," Cerrakin says and eyes him up and down, but before Crazyjones gets to answer, Cerrakin waves it away with his child hand. "Better if I don't know. We need people like you, now more than ever."

"Why?"

"Because our numbers have been dwindling for a long time. And recently our bone assemblers have started disappearing while off retrieving bones. Maybe the incidents have all been accidents, but then again maybe not."

"You have enemies?"

"Plenty," Cerrakin says with a smile as if it was a compliment. "So many enemies that I'll put you straight to work. I would like you to get rid of someone for me."

"I'm no killer."

"I never said kill, did I?"

"And who is it?"

"You tell me."

Chapter 18

Ten minutes later, Cerrakin the Vault Master opens the door and shoos Crazyjones out of it with a smile and a task concerning a vermin infestation in The Vault.

"I'm sure you're up to the task", he reassures Crazyjones. "If not, you might ask Mrs. Sekunda for advice."

Selina Sekunda, who has been waiting by the door, gives a polite nod and Cerrakin addresses her. "Please bring Crazyjones to his new accommodation."

"So he passed the interview," Mrs. Sekunda says, not hiding an undertone of disappointment.

"He did indeed. One of the best candidates in a long, long time. So make sure he feels welcome," Cerrakin says with a smile, but even Crazyjones picks up the veiled threat behind the boyish charm.

At least Cerrakin seems to be on my side.

Selina Sekunda is obviously not, but she nods. "I'll do my best."

"I'm sure you can do better than that, Selina." Cerrakin smiles and then closes the five hinged door to end the conversation.

"Congratulations," Selina Sekunda says, but it sounds more like a condolence.

"Thank you," Crazyjones replies and tries to sound cheerful. "So where are my new quarters?"

"I'll take you there," she says and starts to walk. "It is behind the door with one hinge."

"One hinge? Why just one?" Crazyjones asks and walks side by side with her, trying to be friendly, even if she doesn't reciprocate. "Is there something wrong with the door, Mrs. Sekunda?"

"Mrs. Sekunda," she says with a distaste. Her walk stiffens. "Cerrakin had to point that out, didn't he? But no, there is nothing wrong with the door. You are a one hinger, so you are only allowed to walk through one hinged doors."

"And the other doors?"

"They are barred for your kind. You can knock, but I doubt that anyone will open. And if they do, you better have a good explanation."

"The Vault Master tasked me to get rid of the vermin killing the pigeons. How am I supposed to do that if I can't open any door with more than one hinge?"

"There are no doors inside the pigeon loft. You will stick to ladders, and please secure them before you climb. I don't want to revive you more than I have to."

"I'll do my best," Crazyjones reassures her and changes the conversation. "So how many hinges do you have, M–", but he stops himself in time and ends with, "Selina Sekunda?"

"I'm a three hinger."

"So that is why you knocked on Cerrakin's door? It has five hinges."

"I understand why Miss Huckerpucker chose you," Selina Sekunda says so indifferently that even Crazyjones understands that he must have stepped on her toes.

"I have an affinity with bones," he says.

"That is not the main reason. She chose you because you are like her." Selina gives him an unfriendly sideway glance. "You pry."

"Sorry, I didn't mean to," he says, "but while we are at it, how many hinges does Miriam have?"

"She is a three hinger too," Selina Sekunda says with a self-satisfied smirk. "She lost a hinge when she came in with you on that skeletal raft, and another one earlier this year."

"She used to be a five hinger?"

"Yes, but she sheds hinges like pigeons shed feathers. If she doesn't step up she will end up unhinged."

They walk down a narrow staircase, and Selina Sekunda walks in the middle so there is no room for him at the sides. He has to walk behind her and talk to her back head and the jumping pony tail.

"What happens with the unhinged?"

"The same that happens with failed applicants. It is one of the more satisfactory parts of my job in the mortuary. Putting people down permanently."

"You mean to kill people."

"They are already dead."

"But you like to... put people down? Even your own kind?"

"I used to be a poisoner," Selina says, "but now I follow the rules."

"But you still like it. To... eradicate people?"

"It doesn't matter what I like, as long as I follow the rules. Miss Huckerpucker would be wise to do the same. And you should as well, since you are a one-hinger."

"So what are the rules exactly?"

"For you right now, it is not to pry," she says. "And do as you are told."

"I was told to find a smart way to get rid of the vermin. So I need my dog back."

Selina Sekunda seems like she is reminded of a chore she has intentionally forgotten. "I'll revive him tonight and give him back to you tomorrow."

"Thank you. And if you have a smart way of dealing with vermin, I would appreciate to hear about it."

Selina Sekunda stops and turns around with a smirk. She stabs a finger in his chest.

"Let me tell you how: Unhinge them and put them permanently to sleep," she says and looks Crazyjones up and down. She leaves no doubt of how she sees him, even if she doesn't call him vermin to his face.

Crazyjones has had enough. He chooses to stand his ground and draw a line. That is the best way to deal with bullies. Even if Selina is not the conventional bully.

She is dead after all. And probably far more dangerous than most people.

"You are not the friendly type, are you, Mrs Sekunda?" Crazyjones says.

"I'm sure you'll find a way to deal with the vermin up at the pigeon loft. After all, you are a thinker."

I never said that to her, did I?
Then Crazyjones gets it.
"You were eavesdropping at the door," he blurts out, flabbergasted. "Of all people I didn't expect that from you."
Selina Sekunda's confident and cool composure slips and shows the panic underneath.
I caught her redhanded.
She immediately turns her back on him and walks away at a fast pace, fleeing the scene.
"Wait! Where are you going?" he yells after her.
"To revive your dog," she says without turning. "Your quarters are down that way."
She points down a well lit corridor, then disappears around a corner.

Chapter 19

I got the upper hand.

Crazyjones has a hard time believing he made Selina Sekunda flee the scene, and then he wonders if it was smart to confront her the way he did.

Probably not, but I'll deal with that later. First I have to find my new quarters.

Crazyjones walks down the corridor. At the end there is a one hinged door. A man is standing in front of it, smoking a pipe, and shifts his bored gaze away from an old painting on the wall to gaze full of interest at Crazyjones.

"You are the new guy," he says.

Crazyjones' breath catches in his throat.

The smoking guy's face is ruined, it looks like it has caved in, his teeth rattling as he speaks. "I'm Flatface by the way."

"I'm Crazyjones."

Flatface reaches out a strong hand and gives him a firm handshake. "Welcome to The Vault."

"Thanks. Are you new as well?" Crazyjones asks and tries not to stare at the wrecked face right in front of him.

"No. I lost a hinge, so now I'm stuck with you newbies," Flatface sighs and puffs his pipe. He looks up at the painting, and in profile, Crazyjones sees that Flatface's face is indeed flat.

Crazyjones surmises that he must have fallen from a great height.

Or maybe a full beer barrel rolled off a shelf and hit his face when he looked up.

"So how did you lose it?"

"My good looks or my hinge?" Flatface looks at Crazyjones with a scary grimace that is supposed to be a smile.

"Your hinge."

"Collateral damage," he says and looks back at the painting.

Crazyjones looks up at it as well, to get a reprieve from the destroyed face in front of him.

The painting is of an unhelmed knight standing with one foot on a dragon's head which reminds Crazyjones of Tenderloin the way he looks now. Both creatures have embereyes and the spiky dragon scales look a lot like Tenderloin's new fur. But he suspects the dragon in real life must have been far, far bigger than Tenderloin, even when his dog was oversized for a spell. He envies the dragon its wings.

If Tenderloin had a pair like that it would make the vermin hunt at the pigeon loft much easier.

"He was a great man," Flatface says with admiration. "And no one blamed him for collateral damage."

"He killed the dragon?"

"Embereyes? Yes, he killed the menace once and for all. In the painting the dragon is breathing his last dying breath. Without the fire, of course."

"So who is the man?"

"Have you been living under a rock?" Flatface asks and points with the pipe on the man in the painting. "That is Donnowan Dragonslayer."

Crazyjones hasn't heard of him. Up until now, he has been tending his fields.

"Cheesy name," he says.

"It is a great name for a great man that once was one of us."

"So he is dead."

"You are very new, aren't you?" Flatface says and takes stock of Crazyjones.

"I know that I'm unliving."

"Unliving! Ha, so Selina was the one to revive you. That must have been so much fun," he says without any fun in his voice.

"Are there others working in the mortuary, reviving people?"

"Yes, but most of them left some time ago."

"Why?"

"Because of him." Flatface looks up at Donnowan Dragonslayer. "He vanished without a trace this winter on bone business."

"Sounds serious."

"To make matters worse, he had a contingent of bone assemblers with him, four and five hingers the lot of them. None of them have been heard from since."

"Could it be the pigeon posting system? I heard there were some problems with delayed messages and vermin at the pigeon loft."

"So you are Starion's new replacement."

"Who's Starion?"

"The last newbie that was supposed to do your job."

"And what happened to him?"

"He ran away, I suppose. I bet some girlie hooked him," Flatface says and resets a broken tooth that is almost coming loose. "Starion was a troubadour, one of the stray kittens Miriam brought home. And Starion was a good talker, he first convinced Miriam to convince the Vault Master of his good intentions and work ethic, and then rewarded her gullibility by running away at the first opportunity."

"So why do you think Starion ran away?"

"Because he killed himself in a way that didn't disfigure his body at all. Now he is happily troubadouring the country, knowing that he will be forever young and pretty. And Miriam lost a hinge because of him."

"Because he deserted?"

"No. Because she defended him after he disappeared. Miss Huckerpucker insisted that mischief had befallen him, so much so that it cost her a hinge. She protects her protégés fiercely," Flatface says and looks over at Crazyjones. "I heard you cost her a hinge as well."

"Well, I never meant to."

"Well, neither did I," Flatface says gloomily. "But I lost my hinge anyway."

Chapter 20

Flatface opens the one hinged door to a sparsely lit and sparsely furnished dormitory and introduces Crazyjones to the others, all of them dressed down and relaxing.

"This is Crazyjones, everyone."

"The one that Miriam brought in?" asks a slender female with narrow eyes.

"That's right, Ratty."

"Don't call me that!" the slender female says and walks up to Flatface. "I'm Erina Bulchec."

"You mean the famous thief?" Crazyjones asks. He omits the pretty part, since that is obvious.

Erina Bulchec nods.

"See?" says Flatface. "Even he knows who you are."

"What is wrong with that?" she asks.

"Everyone is supposed to believe that you are dead."

"And I am!"

"You are a reanimated corpse, you stupid gal! If you start strutting around in the city, all hell breaks loose."

"I don't accept Ratty," Erina says and folds her arms. "Besides, I never ratted on anyone."

"Well, don't take it up with me," Flatface says. "It is written in the records. Accept it or die permanently."

Erina sneers and looks around. "If any of you make fun of my name, I will gut you like a fish."

"You are lucky," says a third person, a man with thinning hair and dark circles under his eyes. "I'm registered as Shithole."

"It is actually written Chitwhole," Flatface says. "You can choose to pronounce it Sheet-Owl."

Sheet-Owl lightens up. "Thanks Flatface."

"No problem."

"Then I will be Raithee," Erina Bulchec says.

"It is still written down as Ratty," Flatface replies, knocks some ash out of his pipe and writes her name with his ashy finger on the table. He makes a grin that would have scared all the kids away on Halloween.

A silverhaired and shaggy guy leans over the table and studies the ash written name. "In language mine," he says with a voice like he is singing out of tune, "this letters are said Raithea."

"Raithea," Erina Bulchec repeats after him. "I like it."

Flatface doesn't obviously, and snorts accordingly. Raithea and Flatface stare at each other, both unwilling or unable to yield.

Each of them wants dominion.

"Let's have a vote," Crazyjones suggests and takes the lead. "Those for Raithea, raise a hand."

Crazyjones counts seven, himself included.

"That is a majority," he declares – the only one who didn't raise his hand was Flatface, "Raithea it is then."

"And I'm Sheet-Owl! Let's raise hands to that," says Sheet-Owl.

Everyone except Flatface raises their hand again, and when they look at him, he raises his voice. "I'm not into your stupid games! You will learn reality the hard way soon enough."

"We can have a vote for your name as well," the newly named Raithea suggests. It is meant as a peace offering, but it rubs Flatface the wrong way.

"When we are done, my face will be the pretty one," he says and leaves. When he walks to the door, he intentionally bumps into Crazyjones, but the shaggy silverhaired guy grabs him, preventing his fall.

"Watch yourself," Flatface says without turning. Before Crazyjones can reply, Flatface slams the door behind him.

The tension in the room dissipates.

"Thanks," Crazyjones says to the shaggy guy.

"Me welcome", he answers in a sing-songy way.

"What is your name?"

"Gorthaslaksuranon."

"I didn't get that, I'm afraid.""

"Hello Aididdengethataimafraid," Gorthaslaksuranon says and shakes his hand vigorously.

"He is registered as Northman," Sheet-Owl says. "Gorth Northman."

"Me up north winter snow," Gorth explains. "Me hunt big –"

Then a bell rings loudly.

Everyone sighs simultaneously.

"Mourning class," Raithea says to Crazyjones and hands him a robe, before putting one on herself.

A minute later they walk out in procession through the one hinged door and towards a two hinged door that is wide open.

Chapter 21

An elderly woman with three pairs of spectacles necklacing from her wrinkled neck, head like a woolly sheep and a wooden leg is awaiting the one hingers in a room devoid of furniture.

They walk into the room in silence, circling the elderly woman so that Crazyjones, who was last, ends up next to Raithea, who was first.

It looks like the inside of a die, Crazyjones thinks when he looks at the whitewashed walls with small round windows like portholes on a ship. *Except the numbers on the die sides don't add up.*

"Sit down, please," the woman says.

The one hingers, Crazyjones included, sit down on their knees on the ground. He can see that the others are flustered, eyes darting to and fro, but he doesn't know why.

This is my first mourning class after all. Better lay low.

"Could you please close the door, Ratty?" the wooden legged woman asks Erina Bulchec.

"It is Raithea," Erina replies sternly.

"It says Ratty on the list," the woman answers and holds out the list for them to see. "Go and do as you are told. Close the door, Ratty."

Erina Bulchec refuses, she sits so still that she could have been sculpted in stone. Or be dead, which she is, technically speaking.

"I can unhinge you right here and now," the woman threatens.

But Erina Bulchec refuses to look up at her.

Then Sheet-Owl coughs lightly. His hand has been raised for a while.

"Yes, Shithole?" the woman says and turns to him.

"In the Peccaran language Ratty is pronounced Raithea."

"And?"

"And as aspiring bone assemblers we are required to learn perseverance, tolerance and acceptance of foreign peoples and their cultures."

"Me agree!" Gorth Northman howls in his sing-song fashion and gives a friendly slap on Sheet-Owl's back that sends him sprawling.

"Please refrain from touching in the mourning class, Mr. Northman. That is reserved for gymnastics."

"Me sorry," Gorth says and straightens up Sheet-Owl.

Sheet-Owl smiles and thanks Gorth Northman for his helpfulness and then raises his hand again.

"Yes, Shithole?"

"It is Sheet-Owl. We voted for it."

"Voted? But The Vault is not a mockcracy, my dear Shithole. On the list here it says –" the woman puts on a pair of glasses and reads "–Chitwhole?" Then she sighs. "I'm sure Curan meant Shithole, but whatever! I give in. Otherwise we will never get through the curriculum. I'll call you Sheet-Owl and you stop raising your hand to everything I have to say and I'll call you Raithea," she says and points at Erina Bulchec, "and you do as you are told."

Erina Bulchec aka Raithea gets up and closes the door. Then she returns and sits down as before.

The woman interprets that as an indirect yes and mutters, "Thanks, Raithea." Then she turns to the rest of the class. "Let's start this lecture–"

The door bangs open.

In comes Flatface, not in the robes the others are wearing.

"I'm sorry Curan, I had –" Flatface stops in the middle of the sentence with what must be a baffled expression, had it not been that every expression on his face looks hideous and intimidating. "You are not Curan!"

"Hi, Timeon. Or do you prefer Flatface?"

"You have no right to be here, Pommy Phart."

"I got another hinge," the woman called Pommy Phart announces with a triumphant smile. "Maybe I got yours? I heard you lost a second hinge out on one of your forays."

"Fuck off."

"I tick that comment on your disobedience track," Pommy Phart says and makes a note on her list next to Flatface's name. "You know Selina Sekunda wants to lay you down for good."

"You can tell that stone slab of a woman that she is way too uptight for any kind of laying!" Flatface roars and laughs when no else does.

"Another tick on the disobedience track for making fun of superiors," Pommy Phart says. "You are quite a racer, aren't you Timeon? I bet you could even outpace your horse."

"Keep my horse out of this!"

"Another tick," Pommy Phart sniggers. "And I thought this class would be dull. You have one tick left before you're to be unhinged, Timeon, so you better run and get your robe on and toe the line. Otherwise we will continue this class in the mortuary."

Timeon Flatface makes another face.

It must be a scared expression, Crazyjones thinks, and the second after his suspicion is confirmed.

Flatface bolts out of the door like the little woman was the devil herself.

Before Pommy Phart says anything more, Raithea gets up for the second time and closes the door.

"Thank you, Raithea," Pommy Phart says. "I'll respell your name in the list, so non-Peccarans will get it right as well, and you don't have to raise your hand, Sheet-Owl," she says without turning to Sheet-Owl who is on his way to raise his hand. "I'll change your name as well."

She looks over her spectacles at the class.

"Anyone else who wants a name change?"

Crazyjones raises his hand.

"Yes?"

"I don't need a new name. I just wonder if everyone is allowed to rewrite the lists?"

"Good question, Crazyjones, good question!" She rewards him with a smile that glints of gold. "Let me answer by introducing myself. I'm Pommy Phart, the archivist responsible for the storing and cataloguing of bones and other remnants from the eldest time."

"Oldest," Sheet-Owl corrects, with a raised hand. "Eldest is not a word, not really."

Pommy Phart ignores the comment and continues. "I catalogue what the bone assemblers bring in."

"So as an archivist you are able to rewrite the lists?"

"Correct, Mister Crazyjones." She turns around to the other one hingers. "I'm doing this class as a repayment. Mister Crazyjones added greatly to my collection recently."

"How so?" asks Sheet-Owl, with his hand raised as usual.

"He sailed in on a raft of bones from the eldest time. And because he did that, I'm happy to help him and his friends out."

"Me too!" Gorth Northman howls and slaps Crazyjones' shoulder so hard he falls into Raithea's lap. When he looks up, Raithea gives him a funny smile and says, "You have a strange way of making friends, Crazyjones."

It seems I have been accepted.

Chapter 22

After the fuss with naming and getting Timeon Flatface in line – he sulks in silence following his return, but Pommy Phart ignores him – the rest of the lecture is done in a regular manner.

Crazyjones learns how to sit and mourn his life with his eyes closed.

"It is basically reminding yourself of yourself," Pommy tells him, when she sits down with him. The other ones have been doing this for a while, so they are used to revisiting their living moments.

"So why the reminding?" Crazyjones asks and opens one eye.

"Because you are reanimated," Pommy says with a smile. Both her front teeth are made of gold, and along with her pegleg they strongly hint at a piratical background. "Now be a good pupil and visit some of your memories. Then you will see why you need to do it."

That should be easy.

Crazyjones closes both eyes so hard that there is nothing but darkness. Then he thinks of his annoying neighbour. A shockwave of memories rushes through him and flushes him out of consciousness.

At least that is what he believes has happened when he comes back to himself, opens his eyes and looks up at all the worried faces.

He is lying on his back.

"Did you think about fainting?" Sheet-Owl asks.

"No, but there were so many memories."

"Typical novice error," Pommy explains. "You think of a memory with too many feelings connected to it."

Gorth Northman helps Crazyjones up, while Pommy gives some advice to him that is meant for everyone.

"Think of something simple. Like the cup you used to drink from, or a sign you passed every day to work."

"Like my field?"

"You worked your field a lot, didn't you?" Pommy asks.

"I wanted a good harvest like every other farmer."

"Then no. Too many feelings involved. Think of a big stone or rosebush that bordered your field instead."

Crazyjones sits down to try again. The other ones have already closed their eyes, but one or two open an eye when they think no one else sees.

Must be very boring memories, Crazyjones surmises. Then he closes his eyes again.

He thinks of the blackthorn that he never got to pick for berries to make wine, something he'd promised himself to do every single spring.

The memories come rushing in again, but then slow down to just float by. It is a calm feeling and when someone rustles him, it feels like he has woken up afresh.

He opens an eye.

It is Pommy, both golden front teeth fully visible in her grin.

"You did good, very good indeed."

"Thanks," he says and closes his eyes again to be by the blackthorn, but before he does so he asks aloud: "But what is the purpose of this memorization?"

"Simple. One: To reanimate you. If you let your memories slip, you will wither away as a corpse or fall apart. Two: It makes the spelling class easier when you're not all jumbled up inside."

Crazyjones returns to his blackthorn and he dozes off, but is at the same time still present.

Feels like I am floating… in eternity?

Then some annoying sounds from the outside disturb his peace.

Crazyjones opens an eye again. It is Pommy. She is packing up. Then he realises that all the others are gone.

"I didn't have the heart to wake you from your slumber," Pommy says when she sees he's looking around. "And you will still be in time for your spelling class. Today there was a lot of preparation in that class, so I thought it would do you more good to mourn yourself instead."

She walks out of the room, but stops in the doorway.

"Please close the door when you leave."

"But where are the others?"

"Just follow the smell, and remember to knock if the door is closed. It is a two hinged door and you don't want any ticks on your disobedience track," she says and leaves the room. "Ta-ta."

Chapter 23

Crazyjones walks out the door and closes it as Pommy Phart asked him to do. He can hear her walking down some stairs, her wooden leg reminds him of his grandfather's cane thumping on the floor above, and the memory of it brings a feeling of warm helpfulness.

Strange, he thinks, *I'm not overflooded with impressions.*

But then his grandfather died when he was very young, so he doesn't have many memories of him, and the few he has, blur and then disappear altogether and goes back to Pommy Phart's wooden leg thumping.

"Do you need help, Miss Phart?" he says with a raised but polite voice.

"I'm fine, darling," she answers some distance away. "But I appreciate the gesture."

He listens to her wooden leg get to the end of a staircase and continues caning along a corridor.

Then a smell tickles his nose.

Roasted pig in almond sauce? Another memory of mine?

He takes another sniff.

No, the smell is definitively in the corridor. Pommy said he should follow the smell.

He sniffs around a corner, spirals down a staircase and ends up in a new corridor with a two hinged door.

The roasted pig in almond sauce emanates from the door, along with chocolatey redcurrants drizzled with powdered sweet biscuits and behind them fried tuna chops and marinated venison.

If this is spelling class, Crazyjones wants to do spelling straight away.

He knocks at the door.

"Enter!" someone on the inside shouts.

When he opens the door, a banquet is revealed. A stout man with rolled up sleeves and big burly hands waves him in.

All the other one hingers are here as well, busy putting the different dishes on oval plates.

"I'm Tuddernut," the stout man says and swipes his hands on a cloth before he shakes Crazyjones vigorously. Crazyjones feels like his arm is a hand pump and then suddenly that he is in a foreign country when Tuddernut says some mumbo jumbo.

The next violent shake lifts him from the ground and makes him float through the room.

Am I dreaming?

It is like he is a ship on a light breeze or a scooped out cannonball turned balloony. He sails in a curve, doing a slow flip, before he lands on his buttocks in a chair, followed by a lot of admiring "ooh"s and "aah"s from the other one hingers and a singsong shout from Gorth.

Tuddernut turns to a haughty woman with a noble demeanour that is so striking that Crazyjones is sure that she must be a firstborn nobleman's daughter, and says to her: "That, Braidive, was mixing levitation with paralysis."

The so-called Braidive pretends not to be impressed, so much so that Crazyjones suspects she must be.

Tuddernut says some strange words, does a jump and floats in a curve to land next to Crazyjones.

"And you must be Crazyjones," Tuddernut says with a big smile.

Crazyjones nods.

"This is spelling class."

"It looks more like a cooking class."

"That is because we have diminishing and swelling on today's menu. And what is better than experimenting with food?" He turns to the other one-hingers, instructing: "Gort and Raithea, bring the dishes over, while you Braidive, will be the first to do the swelling."

Braidive comes over and gives Crazyjones a smug smile. "You don't recognize me, do you?"

"No, I can't say I do."

Braidive seems very pleased with that.

"Very good, very good," Tuddernut says. "You sure know your glamour spelling, Braidive. Now take it off."

"But I want to keep it on!"

"It can mix with the other spellings."

"I'll manage."

"If you want to do it the hard way, be my guest." Tuddernut points at a small piece of fried tuna. "Swell it."

Braidive incantates a string of strange words and the tuna piece increases in size and fills the plate, but then something crackles.

Braidive brings her hand to her face. Strange wrinkles have appeared there, and when she furrows her brow, the face breaks off and falls into dust.

Now Crazyjones recognizes Braidive. She has been one of the silent one hingers in the background. She looks hopelessly down at her hands where the dust settles to look like flour, before she sniffles and runs out of the door.

Tuddernut sighs.

"Should I get her?" Raithea asks.

"No. Let her be. In time, Braidive will see this as a good lesson. As I said before, don't spend time being someone else when you're dead. Just be yourself and do the spelling on things that matter."

Sheet-Owl raises his hand.

"Yes?"

"Why do we have this feast when we don't have to eat?"

"But you do."

"Why?"

"It is a good way to remember for one. Taste and smell is more memorable than sight. And when you are out in the field, people will forget you're dead and invite you to dine with them, unless you look like Flatface."

Raithea raises her hand, and Tuddernut nods for her to speak.

"Is that why Timeon Flatface is exempted from today's lecture?" she asks.

"Yes, I want to keep your appetite up as well as mine. Let's swell the rest of the food and eat."

Everyone makes one swelling each, but when they get to the duck breast with sour cherries, Crazyjones is called forth.

"I don't know what to say."

"You incantate Yerra-yerra-dubboli-dub-derram-dwinklehood-astar-yep-sturry while thinking of something increasing in size."

"Incantate what?"

Tuddernut repeats it and adds, "In your case, you can touch the dish. Having a connection makes it simpler."

Crazyjones does as he is told and says aloud, "Yerra-ferra-dubbelidi-dub-derram-dwinklecod-astar-yep-starry!"

The duck breast swells and then sprouts fins as it turns into a living cod. Everybody is amazed, even Tuddernut, but when the cherries start exploding, they all dive down under the table.

When they return from the hiding place, the cod is already shell shocked to death from the explosions and the walls are spattered red from the cherries.

"Works fine in mouth," Gorth Northman says after putting a finger on the spatter to put it in his mouth. "Spicy."

Tuddernut swipes the wall and tastes for himself and nods in acknowledgement. "I think you made a new dish on the fly."

"It reminds me more of a booby trap," Raithea says and keeps a safe distance from the cod.

Chapter 24

Tuddernut walks over to the dead cod and utters new strange words, turning it into a fried cod.

"Let's sit down and eat. And please, dig in, fill your bellies to the brim."

This is a feast, and the tastes bring different memories forth, but they dissolve fast, for Crazyjones has never tasted anything this good and in such abundance.

This is like being seated at a nobleman's table, Crazyjones thinks and digs in.

When the feast ends he feels more like a swollen wineskin ready to burst than an undead apprentice learning magic spells. Gorth is still stuffing himself and speaking in his own language, probably about how good the food is, when Tuddernut rises with a satisfied look. He begins an after dinner speech.

"Imagine that you have feasted at a noble's table. You are out hunting a haunted bone, but hey, the rural noble invites you to get some gossip from the capital and we bone assemblers are supposed to be friendly, right?" Tuddernut looks over at a yawning Sheet-Owl. "The noble invites you to stay overnight as well, but the bone needs picking and you really don't have to sleep, do you now?" but here Sheet-Owl raises his hand. "Yes, what is it?"

"I feel tired."

"It is the memory of tiredness, nothing more," Tuddernut assures him and continues. "But after a few days of hunting bones, something strange happens. You start burping and swelling. What has happened?"

"The noble was in league with the bone and poisoned you?" Raithea suggests.

"Not far off the mark. You are poisoned, but it is self-inflicted. The food has fermented."

"Can't you just puke it out?" Raithea asks.

"You can, but your stomach will still have remnants of food, so unless you want to have a cat's breath and regular rotten foam coming out of your mouth like Selina, you… Yes, Sheet-Owl, what is it?"

"Why does she do that? Dribble black pus I mean?"

"She died of self-poisoning. You awaken in the state you killed yourself. That is why you have a long neck, Sheet-Owl."

Sheet-Owl nods and pulls up the scarf around his neck.

"Can I go back to the tale now, or do any of you have any more questions?"

Crazyjones shakes his head with the rest of the one hingers.

"Thank you. So you eat and act lively when you travel through the countryside and when you are alone you diminish the food to nothing with a simple spell." Raithea is the one to raise her hand this time and Tuddernut sighs. "Yes, Raithea?"

"Why diminish food when you can diminish your enemies to nothing?"

"Because you usually don't have your enemies in your stomach. It is much easier to do spelling on something you have digested, than on something outside of you."

"Me eat enemy?" Gorth suggests.

"Let's try with the food first, Gorth," Tuddernut says. "You can go first. Think of the food diminishing and say gelly-golly-fith-la-folly-umbun-da."

Gorth Northman nods. He throws his head and hair back and shouts: "Nilly-filly-futt-da-dilly-headburn-dad!"

Nothing happens.

Then Gorth Northman's eyes grow wide and he starts to spasm. The next moment everyone except poor Gorth throws themselves under the table while food jets from his mouth and splatters the walls.

Chapter 25

The gymnastics class passes in a more ordinary fashion, except it isn't gymnastics as Crazyjones knows it, but with dull bladed swords. And the gymnastic teacher is a skeletal corpse more scary than Flatface.

Braidive who hasn't shown up, gets a tick on her disobedience track.

She is probably crying her heart out somewhere, poor thing.

Crazyjones feels sorry for her, but that pity turns to himself when the skeletal corpse pairs him with Flatface.

Just my luck.

Flatface's eyes are filled with revenge.

"I heard you and Gorth had a go at the walls in the spelling class and now you have to be the clean-up crew," Timeon Flatface says with his ugly grin.

Crazyjones just nods, he is used to cleaning stables and barns, so food on the wall is a walk in the park.

At least I didn't get a tick on my disobedience track.

Gorth got one, but it was probably because he laughed after emptying himself. And as Sheet-Owl pointed out, it did clean out his stomach, in fact his whole stomach came out inverted, and it took some time to stuff it back in.

The skeletal teacher – Mister Hunt is his name – shows a fencing stance and how they are supposed to move. He picks Raithea as an opponent, and she has apparently used swords before, because Mister Hunt rasps out "good, good" several times, and then turns to the rest of the class.

"And now I want you to practise The Old Swordsman and the Beast, two and two, as I set you up," he says with a creaky voice.

Flatface raises his hand.

"Yes?" Mister Hunt says.

"You paired me wrong, Hunt. A knight is not supposed to fight a simple farmer, it is an insult to my honour."

"I think you lost that honour together with your hinge the other day," Mister Hunt rasps back. "And you are not a knight nor a farmer, but undead."

Mister Hunt looks at them and Crazyjones can clearly see the soul fire burning in his eye sockets.

"Let me at least work with someone at my skill level," Flatface pleads. "I would like to best Gorth or Raithea, preferably both at the same time."

Before Mister Hunt gets to answer, someone knocks at the door.

It must be Braidive.

"Enter."

The door opens and in runs a yapping Tenderloin straight for Crazyjones. Behind him comes Miss Huckerpucker, with a bundle of books hugged to her chest.

Miriam.

"You needn't have knocked," Mister Hunt says and bows elegantly.

"And you don't have to bow to me," she replies with a smile.

"And yet we do," Mister Hunt says and creaks his face in a grotesque smile that makes Tenderloin growl and raise his spiked hackles. Mister Hunt turns to the little angry dogbeast. "And who is this?"

"This is Tenderloin Redeye. He appeared on my last mission, along with Crazyjones," Miriam explains and looks in Crazyjones' direction. "I'm here to pick him up, I mean, not me in person, but, but…"

"It's okay Mirry," Mister Hunt says. "You can have him for whatever he is needed for."

"It's to get rid of the vermin in the pigeon posting system."

"Take him, but please give him a lesson in swordplay when you have some spare time."

Miriam bows and promises to do so. "Mister Hunt, I also brought you the third book in Coffee Shop Mysteries and the fifth in Evil Eye of No Return."

"Excellent! You can leave them by the door. I will pick them up on the way out. Now I have a class to tend to."

Miriam nods and scuffles to the door where she puts down two of the books, but keeps the third. This was the book she lent Crazyjones: The first book in the Earthy Soft Rose trilogy, with the written dedication that was a secret message to him to pass the job interview.

She must have picked it up at the mortuary along with Tenderloin.

Somehow that makes Crazyjones elated. He is filled with a blend of the wistful memories of his grandfather and the blackthorn he never picked and something more when Mirry smiles his way.

"Come on, Tenderloin", she says and the small beast runs towards her, full of energy. Crazyjones follows in tow…

…and Flatface gets his wish fulfilled.

Paired up against both Raithea and Gorth Northman together, and when he refuses – "It was a joke!" – Mister Hunt kindly reminds him of his knightly honour.

"Sometimes I feel sorry for Timeon," Miriam admits when Raithea and Gorth start besting him. Even through the closed doors they can hear the fleshy thuds.

Chapter 26

They walk through an archway, Miriam still holding the book to her chest, like it was a breastplate without back straps.

"Thanks for showing me the way," Crazyjones says, trying to initiate a conversation.

"No problem," Miriam answers without looking up. She walks with small hurried steps with Tenderloin on her heels, the little beast looking up at Miriam every now and then.

Please say something more, Crazyjones wishes.

She doesn't, lost in her own thoughts or maybe hesitant for some reason.

I must have made a fool of myself, he thinks, and then he recalls that she lost a hinge because of him. *She is probably angry at me, or at least at the degradation I caused her.*

Crazyjones has another go at conversation.

"I never got past the dedication," he says and nods to the book she is clutching. "But if yo –"

"You hate me, don't you?"

"Hate you?"

He stops, dumbfounded. She stops as well. Her voice quivers when she talks. "I told you to take this job and now you hate it. And you hate me."

"No," he says, but she clearly doesn't believe it, so he adds: "I'm not the tiniest bit angry at you."

"Sure?" she says and glances shortly up at him before returning her eyes to the floor.

"Very sure. My former life was filled with manure and toil and flies and rain and wolf packs and angry neighbours and whatnot… What are you smiling at?"

"I'm not smiling, at least I'm trying not to," Miriam admits. "But I'm happy that you are not angry about being dead and revived. We need people like you."

But what about you yourself, Mirry. What do you need?

91

His question stays in his head as he never dares to ask, too afraid for the answer.

"You're sure you're not the tiniest bit angry?" she repeats.

"Yes. And I have the best from my former life anyway," Crazyjones says and sits down to pet Tenderloin, "but his fur could be less... spiky."

"He is unique," Miriam says.

"He sure is," Crazyjones chimes in. "Thanks for saving his life. And my life as well. I mean unlife."

"You're welcome. I gave Selina hell for zapping him," she says and hunkers down to pet Tenderloin as well. The little beast must be in heaven, as he rolls over on his back, tongue flapping.

"Zapping?"

"Making something dormant. It's the closest we get to deep sleep and ideal for storage purposes or if you want to experiment on someone."

"Do you think Selina Sekunda planned to experiment on him?"

"I don't know, but she did that with her former husband, at least she was convicted for it, but that was post mortem. She had already killed herself with poison. I think it might have caused her brain damage before death."

"Why?"

"I have never figured her out, she does things I never expect."

"So then we can assume that she didn't zap Tenderloin for experimentation."

"How so?"

"You expected it."

"Hm. Maybe it is just me turning paranoid." Miriam looks up at Crazyjones. "Have the other ones said something?"

"Something about what?"

"Me being paranoid."

"The only thing they have mentioned is that you do unexpected things."

"Ha, you're just trying to be nice. I bet at least one has called me stupid."

"No, they have warned me not to call you stupid to your face. Flatface apparently did that."

"He did and I did lose my temper at that point. Maybe it is because I'm becoming paranoid."

"Relax, Mirry, you're totally okay."

"Nothing more?" she says, and then zips it, like she said something wrong. Her eyes dart down to Tenderloin and her cheeks have a tint of colour in them, when she suddenly says. "You're right, his fur is spiky."

Before he gets to answer, Tenderloin wriggles free from the petting and runs barking down the corridor. They both look after him.

"I hope he is just as effective when we go vermin hunting in the pigeon loft," Crazyjones says.

Ahead of them Tenderloin has rushed around a corner barking furiously as small dogs are wont to do when their owners are nearby.

"Let me take you to the pigeon loft then," Miriam says and when they walk together down the corridor towards Tenderloin's barking, she adds, "I'm glad you're not angry with me."

"Not at all. I would still like to borrow the book."

"You'll find it too soft and romantic. I can find something else."

"At least let me have a go at it."

"Okay," she says and hands him the book.

They turn the corner and stop when they see Tenderloin growling ferociously at a still body halfway through a doorway.

Chapter 27

I know her.
"It's Braidive," Crazyjones says.
Braidive lies in an awkward angle with eyes wide open.
"Poor thing, she has been zapped," Miriam says and sits down at her side. "She must have tried to walk through the three hinged door. She is a first hinger, right?"
Crazyjones nods.
"Then she got a second grade zapping. That is not good. We have to bring her to the mortuary for revival."
Tenderloin has stopped growling and whimpers instead.
"The doors are booby trapped?" Crazyjones asks.
"The right term is spellbound. And she released the spell when she tried to walk through it. I'm just glad it wasn't the one to the right." Miriam looks over at a five hinged door. "If she'd gone through there, she'd have been dust by now."
"Is that why she has a bluish shimmer?"
"What do you mean?"
"Don't you see it?"
"See what?"
"The soul fire that is going through her."
"I can't see soul fire as well as you do, but this is very interesting, and makes me paranoid for real." Miriam waves her hand back and forth, mimicking the soul fire movements. "Like this you mean?"
Crazyjones nods.
Miriam frowns at this new information. "I think Braidive was chased, and tried to get away from someone or something."
"That sounds a bit paranoid."
"My last protégé disappeared suddenly. And he is not the only one."
"Do you mean Starion?" Crazyjones does his best to sound neutral, hiding a hint of jealousy. "I heard he ran away to be the eternal troubadour, melting female hearts on his journey."
"You sound quite troubadourish yourself," Miriam says, smiling.

"But alas, his heart was broken when his true love died and he committed suicide. I revived him because I think his true love was killed and I needed his help in my investigation."

"You knew…this true love of his?"

"Fernina? Yes, she was a bone assembler and an avid bookworm like myself. We used to swap books. She died on the way to a book fair outside of the capital."

"What happened?"

"She got run over by a wagon."

"And that killed her?"

"When Fernina was alive she committed suicide by jumping in front of a wagon. That's the reason she had a silly gait when she was revived to work for The Vault. The easiest way to kill a bone assembler is to hurt them with what killed them."

"But the second runover could just have been an accident."

"It could have passed as one, but the killer forgot me."

"How did he forget you?"

"Fernina received a flyer for the book fair. I never got one." Miriam lowers her voice. "No one else got that flyer either. I checked all the stands and bookstores."

"So the book fair was a sham?"

Miriam nods. "And the killer knew exactly how to kill her. That made me paranoid," she says and strokes her wrists.

"I know I shouldn't ask," Crazyjones says. "But you died of wrist cutting, didn't you?"

Miriam nods. "I am susceptible to both blades and attacks on my wrist. You are susceptible to dog bites and chest wounds."

"Oh?"

"You haven't looked at your chest, have you?"

"Never thought of it before now."

Crazyjones puts a hand inside the robe, and under the shirt.

Tenderloin, who in fact killed him, wags his tail instantly, used as he is to be rewarded when he finds something interesting, in this case, poor second grade zapped Braidive. The little dog looks expectantly at the hand rumbling inside the jacket, knowing his goody pocket is in there.

My chest is not as it used to be, Crazyjones thinks when he checks with his hand. The chest is a little pulpy with a lot of holes. When he retrieves his hand, his fingers drop near-coagulated blood on the floor.

Tenderloin spurts forward, sniffs at the dark red blood, but decides that it is not a snack and that he is probably not going to get one either. His tail stops wagging and his ears flop down, but neither Miriam nor Crazyjones pay him any attention.

"My chest is weird," Crazyjones says at last. "I think all my ribs are broken."

"You'll get used to it. And on the positive side, flexible ribs make it easier to cram through narrow passageways."

She is very positive for one so paranoid, Crazyjones thinks as Miriam returns to Braidive.

And caring.

Miriam closes Braidive's eyes and looks concerned.

"Do you need help –"

But she doesn't. She is concerned with spelling, saying words in a quiet humming way. Soon after Braidive floats up from the floor, limp, with arms and legs hanging.

"I'll bring her to the mortuary and have a check on her myself."

"What do you think happened, Mirry?"

"I think Braidive saw something she was not supposed to see. Then she panicked, ran through the door and got zapped, and whoever it was, wiped her memory with a spell that left the bluish flicker you saw."

"Soul fire. So why didn't I see soul fire in the spelling class?"

"Because the spells at hinge one are very simple. This one is not."

"Why didn't they kill her instead?"

"That would raise suspicion. Had it not been for you, I would have assumed that she just got zapped and when she woke up and remembered nothing, we would have blamed the zapping for wiping her short term memory, scolded her big time, given her two ticks on the disobedience track – this is a three hinged door, she only has one hinge – and put her on penal servitude in the archives or the pigeon loft."

"That is where I am going," Crazyjones says sourly.

"That's true, but it was my idea to put you there."

"Why?"

"Because I trust you. You need to find out what happened with Starion." Miriam puts a finger on the book she has lent him. "You might want to reread the dedication again before you begin reading the book. The author has made some alterations that could cost the author another hinge. But it is better to ask for forgiveness than permission."

Miriam stands up and gives Braidive a push so she floats along the corridor.

"Are you leaving me here?"

"Tenderloin knows the way to the pigeon loft. You just have to ask him. And when you are finished with your chore there, you can ask him to take you home."

"How does he…" but then he sees a faint bluish flicker on his spiky fur. "You have spelled him, haven't you."

She pretends not to have heard and says "You can also ask him to find me. In case you want to read the second book in Earthy Soft." She walks out of the corridor with floating Braidive and disappears behind a corner, but a few moments after she shouts "Happy hunting!".

Chapter 28

Crazyjones sits down and Tenderloin runs up to him, wagging his tail again.

"Take me to the pigeon loft."

"Woof!"

Tenderloin runs down the corridor barking.

"Hey, slow down!"

Apparently, Miriam never thought of that when she spelled him, or the little beast has just shredded his obedience from his former life. The unliving dog slips past a corner, and is out of sight.

At least he is barking.

Crazyjones runs after him, with the book tucked under one arm and with the other lifting his robes so he won't stumble. He is fast enough to see Tenderloin running up a staircase and then onto a bridge over the vault.

Crazyjones follows.

The vault is alight now, and in his side view, Crazyjones thinks it looks like a vast library cum museum. Rows and rows of dusty tomes and bones and artefacts behind glass counters. And people looking up at the barking little thing far above them, and the novice chasing after it.

They all gasp when the little thing jumps from one bridge to another one right under it. And another and bigger gasp follows when the man climbs up on the fence to do the same.

"You don't have to do it!" one robed figure far below shouts.

"You are already dead, you dimwit!" another one yells up at him. "At least let me move away first."

"I ain't aiming for you or the floor!" Crazyjones assures them before he jumps after the barking Tenderloin.

He hits the bridge floor hard, but he yanks himself up and continues the chase across the bridge, into a new corridor, then spiralling up a spiral staircase at least three or four floors, three or more corridors ahead the barking dog stops.

Well, the dog stops, but the barking continues.

When Crazyjones runs through what seems to be a larger archway of some sort, he sees the dog sitting in front of a door. Tenderloin stops barking the moment Crazyjones arrives.

"I think we have to modify the spell Mirry put on you, Tenderloin, maybe slow it down."

"Woof!" Then some tail wagging and door sniffing.

It is a three hinged door.

Better knock.

He has seen what a second grade zapping can do.

Crazyjones knocks.

He hears some muffled sounds from the other side. Then he hears footsteps approaching.

Crazyjones takes a step backwards when the door swings open.

"I said enter!" an irritated woman with goggles and a wide brimmed hat says. The hat is white specked and so is her clothing.

Bird droppings. I'm at the right place.

The woman puts the goggles up on the brow and eyes him.

"So what are you doing here?"

"I'm here to deal with your vermin problem."

"It is not my problem!"

"I didn't mean –"

"And what beast is that!" she says and looks down at Tenderloin.

"It used to be a dog."

"Too red eyed and spiky to be a dog. Does the little monster have a name?"

"Tenderloin."

"Tenderloin," she repeats and Tenderloin wags his tail. She softens and takes off her gloves and lifts him up to her face. "So you are here to hunt vermin as well?"

"Woof!"

"We better find a leash for you," she says to Tenderloin and then she turns to Crazyjones. "You know dogs love bird droppings. Better leash him now, unless you want to practise diminishing spells from today's class."

"Thanks, but no thanks."

"Enter," she says and brings the dog and the gloves into the pigeon loft.

Chapter 29

When Crazyjones walks into the pigeon loft, it's more like entering the bottom of a gorge. The sun shines on the top tiers of birdhouses at least twenty metres up in the air.

The gorge continues as far as he can see in both directions.

"It's huge!" he marvels.

"The crack along the dome is," the woman says matter-of-factly. "The pigeon loft is only around here."

She walks up to a working table where a big man with a hanging head stands next to a cage filled with pigeons. She leashes Tenderloin to a table leg, completely ignoring the man in front of her.

"I just have to dispose of Mister Curan first," she says to Crazyjones. "Then we can take care of the other vermin."

"Mabel, please, you know I didn't want this," the apparent Mister Curan says.

"You told me that you had retired for good," she says and gives him an icy stare that makes him lower his head even further. "Instead you got a new hinge."

"I had nothing to do with it."

"So the hinge just dropped on your head? That at least explains the utter dumbness of it."

"Mabel, please."

"You stopped pleasing me when you gave up your teacher post."

Then it dawns on Crazyjones. Mister Curan must be the teacher that Pommy Phart replaced.

"Mabel, will you listen to –"

"More stupid excuses, Curan?"

Those two have a relationship, that is obvious.

While they continue bickering, and Tenderloin is gnawing on what seems to be a discarded glove, Crazyjones makes himself useful. He finds a broom and starts sweeping the dirt trays around the feeding post.

The few pigeons that are there, scamper, but they don't bother taking flight. While he works, he has an eye on the couple. Mabel gives Curan another scolding as he puts the rack of cages on his back as a rucksack.

"You could at least have told me that you wanted to go hunting again."

"But as I said a thousand times before, I don't want to do that. I think they are short on people, that is the reason."

Mabel puts her hands on her hips. "Or maybe I'm not good enough for you. It is Erina Bulchec, isn't it?"

"Ratty?"

"I heard it's Raithea now," she says and sways her hips. "Wonder how that came about?"

"Says the person who had Starion around!" That must sting, because Mabel is left speechless for a second, and Curan uses the opportunity to hurl further abuse. "No wonder he fled!"

And then Curan bursts out of the room, pigeons cackling in the cage on his back.

Mabel looks devastated, so Crazyjones gives her a moment to recollect herself, while he changes drinking water and replenishes the food trays.

When he is finished, she is able to pretend that she is okay, and with the goggles over her eyes, he pretends not to see they are moist.

"It seems Miss Huckerpucker picked a better candidate this time," she says.

"I used to be a farmer."

"The former one used to be a nobleman and a crybaby and wasn't good for much more than a perch for roosting pigeons."

"I thought they didn't like unlife."

"They liked his songs though," Mabel says, and the way she says it, reveals that she must have liked it as well.

No wonder Curan was jealous.

"I'm Mabel by the way."

"I'm Crazyjones, Mabel."

"Not by the way," she adds. "I'm Mabel Bytheway. We are on

formal terms. Don't want to make anyone think anything of us. There is too much gossiping around already if you ask me."

Crazyjones nods. "So how do you want me to go about this, Mabel Bytheway? The vermin hunting I mean?"

"As vermin hunters do, I suppose. I am no vermin hunter myself. But if you want to make yourself useful, you could fix the leaking roof on the top tier of the pigeon loft. It is leaking water for now, but I suspect it will soon be leaking roof tiles."

Crazyjones looks up, far above him where the sun shines on rows and rows of pigeon holes.

He almost feels like Curan when he looks up.

Defeated.

If I fall I will certainly die, he thinks. Then he remembers he is dead already. But that is a small comfort. *Even if I can't die, I'm gonna hurt myself badly.*

"So the roof leaks, you say? Have you been up there yourself?"

"No, but the pigeons that live there have been shitting on me more than usual."

"And how did Starion go about this when he wasn't a pigeon perch?"

"If it was one thing he did well, it was ladder climbing. That is a part of the troubadouring business, climbing up on balconies and singing songs."

"And how did he disappear?"

"He climbed up that ladder," Mabel says and points at a ladder that is leaned against the wall, "but never came down."

Chapter 30

Crazyjones walks to the ladder, but Mabel Bytheway stops him.

"I'm not stupid you know." She looks at the book he has under his arm. "You can leave the pulp literature at the table here, and read in your spare time."

"I wasn't planning to read."

"And the pigeons weren't planning on shitting on me either," she says and takes the book from him and puts it on the table. A table peppered with bird droppings.

"I would prefer if you could put it somewhere else, Mabel Bytheway. I borrowed the book and would like to deliver it back in the pristine condition that I got it in."

Mabel Bytheway gives it a thought, and then nods. "Fine. I'll put it in the drawer here," she says and retracts a drawer from under the table. She puts the book in and takes a necklace out. "In the meantime, you can have this."

She hands the necklace to him. It is of silver, with an encased knucklebone inside. Crazyjones can see the bone, because of the soul fire it emits through the encasing.

It glows like the bone candle in the Vault Master's office.

"What is this exactly?" he asks as he puts the necklace over his head.

"Behind the encasing? I have no idea. It's sealed. What matters for you is that there is a three hinger spell on it. That means you don't have to knock every time you come running here to hunt vermin."

And you don't have to answer the door. But he leaves those thoughts to himself and nods.

"This is between you and me," Mabel warns him. "If I catch you using it for other doors or you are bragging about it, I can promise you will not regret it for a short time."

"Not regret it for a short time?" Crazyjones furrows his brow. "I'm afraid I don't understand."

"I will have you unhinged straight away. No ticks on the

disobedience track, just a one way ticket to the mortuary. Selina Sekunda is very effective at putting people out of service for good. She doesn't pretend to care, like some others do."

I bet she refers to Curan. Or is it Miriam she is hinting at?

"I will keep this between us, Mabel Bytheway," he promises.

"Good. To show my appreciation, you can call me Mabel from now on."

"Jawohl, Mabel."

"The ladder is there, so hush, hush," she says and shoos him away.

Crazyjones unleashes Tenderloin from the table leg and takes the little beast with him to the ladder. He considers leaving the robe behind, but instead he folds the lower part up and tucks that part into his belt.

The hood is ideal for carrying Tenderloin.

Tenderloin seems to be of another opinion when they start ascending up the ladder. He whines, but he doesn't try to jump ship. Crazyjones climbs quickly up to the lowest tier and grabs a big and sturdy pole, before he dares to look down. He has a bird's-eye view down to Mabel who sits at the table, deciphering a pigeon message and rewriting it on a bigger sheet of paper.

He tries to see what she is writing, but then she suddenly looks up at him, and he pretends to examine the first pigeon hole.

"Starion used the crack to your left to get on the inside."

"Thanks."

She doesn't reply, but continues to watch him.

He moves to his left, clutching at whatever looks sturdy, while balancing on the small ledge layered with bird droppings.

He reaches a crack in the wall.

"This one?" he asks and looks down.

Mabel nods.

Crazyjones puts Tenderloin in the crack before he squeezes through.

"Happy hunting!" he hears Mabel shout from down below.

In front of him, far down the corridor, he sees Tenderloin's emberglowing eyes.

"Tenderloin, come back here!"

"Woof?" The little beast is actually just inside the crack, and now his emberglowing eyes are also looking up at him.

But whose–

When Crazyjones looks down the corridor again, the first pair of emberglowing eyes – the ones in the distance – are gone, followed by a light rustle that sends shivers up his spine.

You were right, Mirry, to be paranoid. Something feels very wrong.

Tenderloin gives an agreeing whimper.

Chapter 31

"We should have brought a weapon," he whispers to Tenderloin. The little beast agrees with a muted bark.

But instead of returning to get one, they continue through the corridor, or the remnants of one. Daylight flickers through holes and cracks in the old walls and the roof, but then Tenderloin bites his leg.

"What are you…"

In front of Crazyjones, the floor has collapsed and the same goes for the floor underneath and so it goes for five more floors. A gaping hole.

"Thanks, Tenderloin."

"Woof."

There is a vertical breach on the wall to the left, and when he looks in, he is met with total darkness. But then he remembers the necklace on the inside of his robe. He takes it out and it bathes the surroundings with a bluish faint light.

I should be able to bypass the hole in the floor if I go through the breach and into…

…a room.

The room on the other side is filled with debris and dust and has probably been abandoned a long time ago.

He squeezes through the breach, getting a sick feeling when his ribs give way, but the feeling is changed into curiosity when he sees three new passageways leading from the room on the opposite wall.

Tenderloin runs into the left one.

"Wait," Crazyjones whispers. He doesn't dare to shout.

He hurries after the dog through the passageway into a small loft room. Tenderloin growls at a corner there, and when Crazyjones holds up his necklace he can see a vermin nest built by rats.

It has been totally trashed, and the rats lie scattered around on the floor. They are not moisty rotten but dessicated like mummies, so they must have been lying here for some time. A couple of them have been ripped apart, leaving dark stains on the floor boards.

It looks like a last stand.

It didn't go well for the rats. Whatever killed them must have been sharp and slashy.

Tenderloin suddenly stops growling. His ears go stiff.

Something rustles on the other side of the wall. Or more like scraping, many sharp objects against the wall.

When Crazyjones retreats, Tenderloin silently follows.

Let's check out somewhere else.

They follow another passageway where he has to lift Tenderloin over some fallen debris. It opens up to the pigeon houses and it stinks. When he looks closer he can see why. Cadavers of pigeons lie around, ripped apart like the rats in the closet. Some of the pigeons have dried up, others have recently been killed and are crawling with larvae and insects.

Crazyjones looks closer at a recently fresh cadaver. He rips off the metal tube on the leg and holds it up in a stream of daylight when he opens it. It contains a message, scribbled so small that it is impossible to read in the faint light. He tucks the messsage back in the metal tube.

No wonder they have had delays in the pigeon posting system. A killer is on the loose here. And when it can rip apart a pack of rats, I should at least make some preparations for the next time I go hunting.

He collects all the metal tubes he can see, before he returns the way he came. But when they get to the debris strewn part of the passageway, Tenderloin stops at a hole in the wall on the opposite side of the pigeon housing.

"What have you found?"

"Woof?"

"Let me have a look then."

Crazyjones bends down as he looks into the hole. It is totally black, so he gets his necklace out and holds it in front of him.

It seems to be another room and more debris. Then he sees that the debris in the middle of the room has the shape of a man. It is too far away to reach, and the hole is far too small to get through.

Then he hears scraping from somewhere near.

Suddenly he feels like he is in danger. The feeling is reinforced by Tenderloin scuffling onto his back and into the hood.

They retreat silently, but when Crazyjones comes out into the open and climbs down the ladder with Tenderloin still in his hood, he feels that he might have exaggerated the situation. Perhaps it was only debris after all, and he just imagined it was a man lying there. He has done that plenty of times in the forest in the dusk. Imagined things. Trees take untreelike shapes. Sounds swell. Scraping from branches sounds like the scraping you would think the monster under the bed would make.

When he was a child, his parents told him that there were no monsters.

Now he has one in his hood. And probably one in the pigeon loft as well. But he leaves the speculation to himself and pastes a smile onto his face before he walks over to Mabel.

Chapter 32

"Finished with today's work?" Mabel Bytheway says when he steps off the ladder.

"I found a rat's nest."

"And?"

"They were long dead."

"And not resurrected, I assume?"

"No. How so?"

She prims up her mouth. "You have to work on your work ethic. Half an hour's work is nada, considering you're dead and don't have to eat, sleep and shit, like some others have to do," she says and looks at the food post where pigeons are busy doing both. "For some reason more comes out of the pigeons than what goes in. I call it pigeon magic."

"It is more than that. It's market magic."

"And what is that exactly?"

"Guano is worth a lot."

"Guano?" she asks and hoists her goggles on the brow. She is peering at him from under her wide brimmed hat.

"Fancy name for bird droppings," Crazyjones explains and adds: "It is worth a lot."

"You are pulling my leg."

"No. It gives the crops a good yield. Farmers are wild about it. Dogs also, unfortunately." Crazyjones still remembers how Tenderloin managed to stuff himself on it when he was a puppy, got sick and had to be taken care of for a week. Instead of getting a good crop that year, he got a lousy one, tending to his sick puppy dog. "By the way, have you seen Tenderloin?"

"He is in your hood still."

"Oh? Thanks." He puts Tenderloin on the ground and Tenderloin walks to the nearest table leg and lifts one of his hind legs.

Nothing comes out.

Mabel pities him and gives him a ruffle with her gloved hands.

"Sorry dear," she says to Tenderloin. "That is a part of being undead." Tenderloin doesn't give up that easily, but has a go at another table leg. But when he is not able to mark that one either, he sits down, confused.

"Anyway, I'm not gonna sell guano," Mabel says in a decisive voice, but her body language reveals an interest in doing just that.

"Then I'm not gonna tell you that the market price is at least eight shillings a pound."

"Eight shillings you say?"

Crazyjones nods. Tenderloin tries to mark Mabel Bytheway's right boot, but his rear apparatus is unsuccessful. Not a drop comes out.

"If this is a joke," Mabel says, "it is a three-tick-joke on your disobedience track."

Considering the last threat of sending him straight to the mortuary, he interprets the warning as being on her good side.

Better work while the iron is hot.

"I have something more up my sleeve as well."

"More guano?" she says with money-grubbing eyes.

"No, this," he says.

Out from his sleeve roll all the tubes he collected from the dead pigeons. Her eyes widen in disbelief.

"It must be at least twenty tubes."

"And that was only the top tier," he says triumphantly.

But then he understands she is agitated the wrong way, not guano-happy, but so furious that her hat falls off when she lifts her head and nails him with her stare.

"You stupid halfwit! Do you realise how many hours of extra work you have just given me!"

Chapter 33

With an angry shout Mabel Bytheway throws the tubes in his face. They drizzle like overgrown pellets on the floor and dozens of pigeons flock around him, plonking on the metal tubes.

Crazyjones feels like Curan with the pigeon cage rucksack when he receives an iron hot and fiery scolding about him being stupid and Mabel Bytheway being overworked and there is no payment for overtime by the way, she complains as she chases him off the ground and through the door, and the Vault Master doesn't allow unions and scoffs at worker rights and minimum wages –

She slams the door in his face.

That could have gone better.

He looks down at Tenderloin who is trying to pee on the door frame and feeling sorry for himself when he doesn't succeed.

Tenderloin looks up, giving him the sad doggy eyes, but doesn't succeed at that either since the eyes are fiery and emberglowing.

So he whimpers instead.

"I know, I know. It is a new world, but it is our new world as well, so we better get used to it. At least we have a home–"

"Woof!"

Tenderloin's legs turn into drumsticks as he chases along the corridor barking.

Oh no, I said home.

Miriam's spell must have activated at the word "home", but before the beast gets far, Crazyjones manages to step on the leash so Tenderloin stops abruptly, though his legs still run as possessed and the barking continues.

I wouldn't mind a walking and silent mode, he thinks as he grabs the leash and follows after the little beast. Tenderloin tugs at the leash so hard that the dog is mostly walking on two legs, strangling his own barks in the process.

But being undead means that he doesn't really need to breathe, so Crazyjones doesn't feel sorry for him, just happy that the barking is muffled. On the walk home he turns around at every junction to memorise the way, but he doesn't bother counting the doors since they don't go through any. He appreciates that Miriam thought of that, even if he has a necklace now that allows him through doors with up to three hinges.

If not more, Crazyjones wonders. Not that he is going to try. He doesn't want to end up like poor Braidive.

When they walk onto a bridge over the vault, he can see the people down below packing up for the day. The daylight above him that shines through a dome of rounded glass reinforced with thick iron bars, is waning.

Soon it will be evening.

Strange. It feels like I have been here a year, but I haven't been here for a full day yet.

The people below him seem disinterested in their surroundings, used to being in an undead state. They talk with hushed voices, roll up scrolls that they have been studying during the day and put bones back in their glass cases. A senior with a chain of keys locks the cases and a couple discuss the muffled barking nuisance on the bridge above.

"Must be one of the newcomers, a one hinger for sure," Crazyjones hears one of them say to a colleague, before they trot off, following the same path between the bookcases as they came in, not a bit interested in finding a new way.

Crazyjones remembers that his grandfather used to say "Happy is the man who sees the world anew every day", and he feels kind of happy being here, overlooking the new world that he has been thrown into.

They pass the bridgework and follow corridors, through archways and up and down stairs with a constant muffled barking and stopping at regular intervals to turn around to memorise the surroundings better, before they end up in front of the door with the one hinge.

Tenderloin instantly stops barking as soon as he reaches the door. He looks exhausted, panting with his tongue. But when the dog realises he is not tired – he is undead after all – he tries his rear apparatus on the door frame with new gusto. His hind leg goes up and down as a hand pump, but not a drop comes out. He looks up at Crazyjones, almost accusingly.

"Don't give me that look. You killed me, remember, not the other way around. Be positive. Your well might have dried up, but at least there are no butterflies here."

Maybe there are needled butterflies behind the glass counters down in the vault, undead butterflies might exist for all I know, but Crazyjones doesn't say that out loud.

Behind the one hinged door a mishmash of voices comes through. Crazyjones hears Gorth Northman roaring with laughter.

He opens the door to see Raithea and Gorth sitting by the table, swapping to puff on Flatface's pipe, both with content expressions, while Sheet-Owl and two other one hingers reenact today's events with funny grimaces and broad gestures in front of them.

Apparently those events didn't go well for Flatface, for he is nowhere to be seen.

Chapter 34

The other one hingers are in a great mood, and while Raithea and Gorth continue puffing on the peace pipe – *they seem to like each other* – the last three of them replay the fight in the gymnastics class.

"You could see Flatty regretted it straight away," a one hinger called Funix says and then turns to one of the others. "It is your time to play Flatty, Dimly."

"Okay," Dimly says with a shrug. Crazyjones suspects the nickname fits with his apparently slow thinking, and Funix with entertaining humour.

Before they start the show – Raithea has put out a chair for Crazyjones to sit on – Crazyjones asks Funix, "You were an actor before?"

"Sort off," he says and shrugs it off. "Let's start."

"He was a gutter rat," Raithea whispers as Crazyjones sits down next to her. "Doing odds and ends."

Crazyjones nods, but it doesn't make him any wiser – *but whatever!* – and he decides to enjoy the show.

The gist of it is a reenactment of how Raithea and Gorth bashed Timeon Flatface, now nicknamed Flatty. Gorth battered him big time with the sword, while Raithea managed to get around his back to manhandle him.

"Clever," Crazyjones says, without really meaning it. If Gorth Northman had come grizzlybearing at him, he wouldn't be too concerned with his surroundings. Crazyjones is more impressed by how Timeon Flatface managed to ward him off for such a long time, but that is an opinion he keeps to himself.

It ended when Raithea bashed his face in on a bench again and again, until Mister Hunt dragged her off him. Sheet-Owl who plays Raithea shows this by bashing Dimly's head in a pillow while Funix is roaring in the background pretending to be Gorth.

Funix must do a good job, because Gorth is puffing contentedly on his pipe. He even offers Crazyjones a pull of the pipe, after Raithea

115

nods in acknowledgment.

"Thanks," Crazyjones says and takes a pull. The smoke makes him feel alive with the memories of his grandfather who used to smoke pipes. He hands it over to Raithea next.

"Two distract," Gorth says when Dimly – at Sheet-Owls order – goes limp.

"You two distracted him?"

"No, we got two ticks on the disobedience track," Raithea explains.

Gorth nods and tries again. "This-to-be-dense-track?"

"You are getting closer, Gorth," Raithea says and then continues the conversation with Crazyjones. "We got one tick for bashing his head in. That made him dormant, so now he lingers in the mortuary, waiting for revival. And one tick for taking his pipe."

That doesn't sound too good, Crazyjones thinks. Both Raithea and Gorth are bound to get more ticks soon, troublemakers as they are.

"Before you ask, yes, it was worth it," Raithea says, like she is reading his thoughts. "He called me Ratty. The sorry part is that he is probably back up tomorrow."

"Not necessarily," Crazyjones says. "Braidive got zapped on a three hinged door, so she needs revival as well."

Everyone turns to him, interested. Crazyjones retells the events, skipping the part of Braidive being spelled and probably chased, and instead hinting at her being so distressed that she forgot herself.

"It can happen to anyone," Sheet-Owl says. "I would have been zapped today, if Raithea hadn't stopped me opening the door to the spelling class."

"Old habits die hard," Raithea says and then turns serious. "Bet Curan will revive Flatface first, he showed him a lot of leniency and goodwill in mourning class."

But Crazyjones shakes his head. "Curan is out delivering pigeons, so I think not," he says matter-of-factly and snaps another puff on the pipe. "Only Selina Sekunda is down there, and as Pommy said, she wants to lay Flatface down for good. She has a beef with him."

"And probably a lot of other people want to take a slice of Flatty as well," says Funix. "He was well hated when living."

"Did you know him?"

"Not personally," Funix says, "but I was at the trial. He was Timeon the robber knight, also known as Blackheart. A big time murderer, blocking bridges and murdering innocents trying to pass."

"The serial knight?" Sheet-Owl asks.

Funix nods.

"You said you were at the trial," Crazyjones says.

"Of course, they were going to gut him and hang him and whatnot."

"That is not suicide. I thought that was a condition to work in The Vault."

"So it is, so it is. Everyone wanted to see him executed so they did it from the clock tower. But he threw himself off the tower before the execution." Funix smiles. "I use that memory in mourning class to cheer up."

"Why?"

"He hit my father before bashing the ground. After that my father never hit me again," Funix says with a grin, displaying plenty of brown teeth and black holes.

I probably had a good life compared to Funix, Crazyjones thinks. *The only fun thing for him was probably his name, if that was his name in real life.*

"So how was your day?" Raithea asks Crazyjones.

"You mean apart from cleaning dirt trays and feeding pigeons? There was some climbing and finding that there is in fact vermin in the pigeon loft. Whatever it is, it has killed a lot of pigeons and wiped out a rat's nest. And those rats were quite big." He turns to Raithea. "You don't have a weapon I can borrow from you?"

"Why would I have one?" she asks.

"I heard Erina Bulchec was an ace with daggers and smallswords, drawing faster than any city guard."

"Still do," she says and all the others gasp when she says that. Then Crazyjones looks down and he realises he has a dagger to his throat.

"That dagger... looks smart," is all Crazyjones can say.

"If I lend it to you, my debt is paid," Raithea replies.

"What debt?"

"Don't play dumb. You helped me get the name Raithea so I owe you." She sheaths the dagger and hands it to him. It is an exquisite piece of workmanship. "Promise to take good care of it. The dagger was dedicated to me by my mentor, he even carved the dedication into the hilt here."

She shows him, but Crazyjones suddenly remembers Miriam's new dedication in the Earthy Soft Rose book. The book is still in the drawer in Mabel's working table.

And I forgot to read it.

He scrambles from the table, gives a hurried thanks for the dagger and runs out of the door with Tenderloin in tow.

Chapter 35

Even the dead are silent in the night. The passageways have somehow been dimmed, the lamps only burning with a small flame. Their flickering reminds Crazyjones of distant bonfires on black hills, too far away for the sound to reach him. He slows down to concentrate more on the route back to the pigeon loft, and also because a running man can be heard from afar.

I have to remember the way.

Asking Tenderloin for help will let loose a barrage of barks and wake up the whole Vault.

He turns to the dog.

"Come here," he says and lifts him up and puts him in his hood. "You can keep watch over our rear."

Tenderloin gives a short yap, in acknowledgement or because he likes to be up in the heights overwatching.

Crazyjones starts walking, thinking of the blackthorn he never picked and his grandfather. It calms him, and makes it easier to navigate The Vault. When he finds himself on the same bridge that they crossed when returning from the pigeon loft, he is pleased.

The big domed room is now a vacated black hole. Except for the night sky that shines through the glass dome and some bluish flickers far below him, it is dark, so dark that he brings out the necklace to light up the way.

As he stops to get the necklace out, he peeks down.

The bluish flickering below emanates from the glass counters.

Probably soul fire from the bones there, blurred by the glass or spells or both.

He holds out the necklace as a light source in front of him and crosses the bridge. On the other side, he is once more in a maze of passageways, walking gingerly and scanning his surroundings.

Up and down, in and out, trying to imagine how everything he memorised would look in the dark and breathing in relief half an hour later when he stops in front of the three hinged door to the pigeon loft.

Tenderloin rumbles softly. He must be asleep or in deep slumber or whatever undead monsters do when they rest.

Hope the necklace works...

He opens the door slowly, takes a deep breath, and walks through waiting for an instant zap.

Nothing happens.

It worked!

A little bit shaky and at the same time very happy for not getting a second grade zapping, he looks around.

Mabel Bytheway has retired from work. He was afraid she would work overtime, but obviously she is as workshy as he suspected. When he walks over to the drawer and opens it – there's a lock, but the key is in it – he finds all the pigeon tubes tucked in there, unopened. The book lies there as well, still in pristine condition. He takes out the book, opens it and reads the dedication, muttering the words to himself.

"In case of emergency, you can say to yourself bee-kjuut-width-aaalight-embrais (sounds almost like be-cute-with-a-light-embrace) and then think of a mule kicking (the spell is self-invented and is called the mule kick). That should send whatever threat approaching you flying. You should practise it a couple of times in total secrecy, with a ball or something. Not glass. Not under any circumstances Tenderloin. PS! I think there is a traitor among us and I also think I'm paranoid. I would write more, but there is no more..."

He turns the page.

"...room on the previous page."

Crazyjones smiles to himself.

Mirry, you are one of a kind.

He silently pushes the drawer in when he hears light thumping.

Knocking?

Crazyjones sees a figure at the door and quickly dives behind the working table. He tucks the necklace inside the robe to hide the soul fire.

The figure is speaking softly.
But to whom?
Then he hears flapping.
From the starry night a black shape lands in the middle of the room with a clawing sound. The man-sized creature doesn't have feathers. It is scaled.
And its eyes glow red.
Crazyjones goosebumps.
The creature looks like a miniature version of the dragon in the painting of Donnowan Dragonslayer. And when he comes to think of it, Tenderloin looks a lot like a miniature of the miniature dragon now perched in front of them.
Luckily his little beast is in dreamland, doing a miniature version of snoring that cannot be heard, only felt against his upper back where the hood and Tenderloin's body presses against his.
The dragon opens its mouth and Crazyjones hears hissing and the clanking of fangs.
"He found Starion, you say?" someone asks. "Then we have to get rid of the pryer."
Another hiss and the sound of sharp teeth colliding.
"No, we do it the smart way. I have an idea that I have already tried. Everyone thought Braidive acted stupid. But she will seem smart compared to Crazyjones."
The dragon's mouth produces an even more infernal sound.
"Yes, you can eat his little beast afterwards."
Crazyjones feels a mix of intense fear and anger. He draws Raithea's knife, and instantly regrets it. When unsheathed, the blade makes a barely audible singing sound, but the dragon creature's ears pick it up instantly..
It swings its head towards the working table.
With a mighty flap of its wings it lifts up in the air and lands seconds later with a big thump on the table, flaring its nostrils and baring its teeth, sending Crazyjones scurrying backwards and waking Tenderloin in the process.

When Tenderloin sticks his head up to see what they are up against, he flees from the hood and runs under the table, and the dragon swings its head in the direction of the dog. That gives Crazyjones the opportunity to take a swipe at the dragon creature. It easily evades the blade, and whips him so hard with its tail that he smashes into the wall loud enough to make several pigeons fly up from their resting places.

"Shhh!" the figure at the door hushes. "Do you want to wake up the whole Vault?"

The dragon sneers at the figure and says: "You are losing power over me, manling," in a human guttural voice.

"I'm your master."

"Not my true master. In time I might devour you. Now I will devour the manling here."

"No."

It is not the figure at the door, but Crazyjones who says it. He has risen and holds the dagger in front of him.

"You have one fang," scoffs the dragon creature. "I have plenty."

It smiles with a whole spectrum of fangs.

But that is exactly what Crazyjones hoped for.

A distraction while he incantates.

"Be-kjuute-with-aaalight-embrace!"

He thinks of a mule kicking super hard.

And succeeds.

But the wrong way.

The dragon creature is not flung away, but flung at him at full speed.

It emits a terrible shriek when the dagger impales its chest, then slams like a cannonball into him and crushes Crazyjones' already pulpy chest in the impact.

"Miriam!"

Her name is the last word that escapes his lips before he enters oblivion.

Part 3: Countdown with Miriam
Chapter 36

Grounded.

I was really looking forward to this. Jump into bed and binge-read the third and fourth book in Evil Eye of No Return, but Crazyjones distracts my mind. My heart goes thump-thump every time I think of him, which is both irritating and pleasing at the same time. Irritating because I have to reread the sentence where the thump-thump occurred and pleasing because I found one with affinity for seeing soul fire, and –

Yes, one of my more sinister thoughts says, waiting for me to think more.

No, nothing more, I think. *I'm just happy on a professional basis.*

Or the rushed romantic in you is on a new and great adventure, the sinister thought suggests.

Don't you get it, you evil and stupid thought! He has the affinity for seeing soul fire!

And you have the affinity for thump-thumping yourself into trouble, the sinister thoughts replies and shuts the door on me.

I hate it when my thoughts show up unannounced like that! And I am starting to hate the third book in Evil Eye of No Return, because it reminds me of my unannounced thoughts. I remember my mourning classes where we were told to sit and wait for the thoughts to come. But when those thoughts know you're waiting for them, they never bother showing up.

And book three in Evil Eye of No Return is exactly like that. The last two hundred pages it has been promising to catch the villain, but he never shows up.

And that is just like in real life!

I throw the book away, lock Crazyjones out of my mind and try to think of other things I don't want to think of, like Fernina's permanent death and Starion's disappearance. I don't like to think of them because they 1) make me sad, 2) make me feel guilty somehow and 3) because I know in my gut that they are not accidental.

Someone is pretending to be someone they are not, a thought in me says, but that is not very helpful unless I have an idea of who that someone might be. It would have helped if I was allowed to study the big skeletal hand I rafted in on, but access is restricted to four hingers and above.

I suspect King Kiddo snapped one hinge off me for exactly that reason. King Kiddo is what we oldtimers call Cerrakin the Vault Master between ourselves. When I asked Tuddernut about his opinion of why I lost a hinge, he said it was because 1) if I hadn't I would have kept the skeletal hand to myself – which I admit is partly true, I've heard plenty of times that I am territorial – and 2) the whole thing would probably blow up during my experimentation so the only thing left of The Vault would be the crack where the pigeon loft is. When I said that that didn't make sense, a crack cannot stay on if the wall it is cracking disappears, he said 3) that King Kiddo cannot make sense of me either. When I inquired what he meant by that, he said that I was borderlining between stupidity and ingenuity. When I asked what he meant exactly, he said 4) that I also asked far too many questions and should have joined Donnowan Dragonslayer and the other four and five hingers on their travels up north.

I don't think he meant it in an evil way – after all, we have heard nothing from them since snowfall, almost half a year ago. When I asked Selina Sekunda what she thought about the missing expedition, she said she still doesn't want to be friends with me. I'm too nosey for her taste.

And Mabel Bytheway pretends to be busy every time I show up at the pigeon loft, even if we both know that she is slacking. She spends most of her time quarrelling with Curan, who doesn't give her enough affection, or complaining of poor wages and never ending chores. The only time she shuts up about the money issue is when Selina Sekunda is around. Selina has volunteered to put Mabel out of her misery for good.

I'm filled up with these kinds of thoughts, when I suddenly hear barking in the distance.

I get out of bed and when I open the door Tenderloin jumps right at me so fast that he scatters all my ponderings.

Thump-thump.

Crazyjones?

I look out of the corridor. But it is dark and empty. No Crazyjones to see or even hear. Just emptiness and stillness. And low whimpering from Tenderloin who shelters behind my feet, exhausted and afraid.

This is all wrong, my gut feeling says.

I grab my sword and say to Tenderloin: "Take me to Crazyjones."

The whimpers are replaced with loud barks and the next moment the little beast is chasing down the corridor he came from.

Chapter 37

It was smart to include Crazyjones when I put a wayfinder spell on Tenderloin. It would have been even smarter to include a silent and walking mode in the spell, but I didn't have time for that.

Now I barely have time at all if I'm to keep up with Tenderloin on a wild goose chase to I-don't-know-where. I only know the target, Crazyjones, but he could be anywhere, so I yell at Tenderloin to stop to no avail and he is barking back so we must be waking everyone on the way. It is true that the dead don't sleep, but we recuperate which is almost the same thing. You learn it in mourning class. For me it was a natural thing. Throwing spells also came easy, but listening to theory wasn't that easy. Tuddernut admitted later – when we were colleagues – that I was his best and worst student. He was relieved when I passed class without blowing the classroom to bits.

I don't know how he got the idea that I like to blow up things.

A sneaky thought comments: *What about the kitchen incident and–*

Shut up, you stupid and sinister thought! I'm trying to catch up with Tenderloin. I hope nothing has happened to Crazyjones.

In the next moment my heart goes thump-thump and that distracts me from further thoughts. I chase the little beast along a bridge over the vault with my sword in hand – still sheathed, I never got time to buckle it on the belt – when the little bugger suddenly sidetracks off the bridge and jumps down to a lower one. The fall is far enough to make his legs sprawl out like a starfish – including a howling yelp of pain – and for me to curse myself for not including a prohibition to hurt himself on the spell I cast on him.

Partly yelping and barking, he gets on his small paws and races over the bridge. I don't think, but jump after him, and manage to land on my feet running so I actually close in on him.

But when I hear a glass counter shattering down below me, I suspect it must be my sword, no longer in hand. Only a flapping sheath. The sword must have slid out in the fall. A quick side glance reveals a glass counter down in the vault sending blue sparks from a big bone that has been impaled on what unfortunately looks like my sword.

King Kiddo is going to be furious with me, but I have no time for damage control, I think to myself, *and the bone is impaled, so it's not getting anywhere... I hope.*

I'm just a few metres away when the bridge ends and we pass through a big archway, and Tenderloin sidetracks again, this time running into a small hole. I run straight at it, yelling "Gelly-golly-fith-la-folly-umbun-da!"

My hair brushes the top of the hole as I instantly shrink and learn a new and inventive way to I-don't-know-where. With me being so small, Tenderloin looks like the beast he once was, but stockier. And with four legs he is increasing the distance between us.

Next time I do a wayfinder spell I have to take size and shortcuts into account, I think to myself. I have only done it on horses before, and they are bigger, not smaller than humans. And on horseback, speed or size doesn't matter that much since you are supposed to sit on their backs.

Tenderloin's tree trunk-like legs thunder through a small tunnel and shortly after we are back in a more expansive space. The passageway we run into looks enormous until I yell "Yerra-yerra-dubboli-dub-derram-dwinklehood-astar-yep-sturry!" and grow large again, which is quite small compared to standard human size.

As we come upon the door to the pigeon loft, I realise where we have shortcutted to. The door is open and Tenderloin runs straight in. Did Crazyjones have a falling accident?

But why is he working here in the middle of the night?

I run through the three hinged door and see only dark silhouettes against the twinkling night sky. Tenderloin scuttles into the darkness and suddenly stops both barking and running, having reached his destination.

I know the pigeon loft quite well, having had a couple of stints there for different reasons, and with my eyes adjusting to the darkness, I can see the shape of Mabel's work bench – it has toppled over and is laying on its side – and behind the bench, close to the wall I find Crazyjones' crushed body next to a sprawling... eagle?

The eagle thing is already decomposing, emitting flurries of stinking vapours that make me think of rotten food churning with maggots and buzzing with flies.

This makes no sense!

Then by chance I see something furry, actually I see something blinking first, a slim and long dagger that has stabbed a furry thing in the middle of the chest of the rotting bird carcass.

I pick up the knife and look at the furry thing.

It is not a rat as I first suspected, but a rabbit's foot, just like the one Tenderloin is spellbound to.

"Woof!" Tenderloin barks and looks at me with his glowing embereyes. He seems very concerned with his master.

As should I.

"Sorry, I'll have a look at him straight away," I say to Tenderloin and hunker down beside Crazyjones. "Crazyjones?"

No answer.

His chest looks caved in, just like Flatface's face, and it must have killed him, but not in a permanent way I hope.

I put my hands on his chest to check on him, but as soon as I touch him he zaps me big time. An electrical jolt runs through my body and everything turns dark.

Crazyjones, what have –

Thump-thump, I think my heart replies from far away.

Chapter 38

I wake with a jolt, still in my rushing mode.

I have to save Crazyjones!

My heart replies with a thump-thump, but when I try to rise, someone holds me down.

"In a hurry, are you?"

A blurred small figure stands in front of me, and a big blurred figure is pressing me down in the chair someone has placed me on.

I'm in big trouble, I think.

Don't blame me, a sinister thought thinks back. *If you identified more with me instead of the rushed romantic part of yourself, you wouldn't have been here.*

But...

Fix your own mess, then we might talk, the sinister part of me thinks, and then leaves.

My eyes blink a couple of times.

I get a clearer view of the surroundings and realise that I'm in bigger trouble than I had first expected.

I'm not taken hostage by some evil villain.

I'm in the Vault Master's office. The small figure is King Kiddo himself and the man holding me down is Ol'Blindeye, King Kiddo's manservant.

Better be on the offensive. And not say King Kiddo, from now on I will stick to Cerrakin or Vault Master.

"Someone zapped me!" I cry in defence.

"So you've finally decided to wake up," Cerrakin says and looks at something next to me.

There, on a nicely carved pedestal, is my sword, standing upright and currently busy impaling a bone that emits flickers of soul fire. The sword runs through the pedestal as well.

"I can explain, Cerrakin."

"Don't Cerrakin me," he sneers. He must be pretty pissed off because he looks like an eight year old brat that only got soft presents

129

for Christmas. "Until I say otherwise, I'm Vault Master Cerrakin to you."

"Of course, Vault Master... Cerrakin."

"That will do, for now," Cerrakin nods and looks up behind me. "Release her, please."

Ol'Blindeye, with his glazed eyes and firm, but careful grip, lets go of me and goes back to pick shards of glass off the pedestal. Cerrakin the Vault Master goes behind the office table to sit on his three pillowed puffed-up chair to get to my eye level, leans his elbows on the table and steeples his fingers.

"Explain."

"I got zapped when I ran to rescue Crazyjones and someone must have put a spell on him, just waiting for me to touch him –"

Cerrakin lifts a finger and I shut my mouth, even if I don't want to.

"You sound kind of paranoid, Miss Huckerpucker. As I see it –"

"But–"

The Vault Master gives me a steely stare, the kind that does not belong to a boy, but to an ancient man.

"Sorry, Vault Master Cerrakin."

"As I was going to say, considering the circumstances caused by your impatient behaviour, I will call this even."

I'm dumbfounded, and not at all able to hide it, so he continues. "You seem surprised."

"I am... Vault Master Cerrakin. I don't think you grasp the whole situation."

"I think I do. You recruited a new protégé, set a new record of killing protégés, the previous was six days by the way, now you managed to do it in less than twelve hours from revival, but also got rid of the menace in the pigeon loft."

I furrow my brow to show I disapprove. After all, I'm not allowed to talk unless spoken to.

"I can see that you don't agree and against my better judgement I will hear you out. From my perspective, this is what happened: you caused quite a ruckus, thrusting your sword through glass counters and old bones, put your protégé in danger by assigning him to deadly tasks outside work hours, the last one, Starion, probably fled because of that, but you also killed off a bird of prey that has been preying on our postal service for a long time and that means you lose one hinge and get one and we will leave it at that although I'm impressed that you haven't interrupted me once."

"Hmpf."

"You are angry?"

"No."

"You are not angry?"

"Yes."

"You are not even listening to me."

"Hmpf."

Cerrakin slams his hand on the table so hard that I wake up from my daydreaming – daysulking would be a more appropriate word in my case – and Ol'Blindeye stops picking shards.

"You're grounded!"

"I'm already grounded."

"Then it's permanent!"

"That's not fair!" I say and stand up.

"Life is not fair. Better learn it while you can."

"But I'm dead! And you are wrong!" Before Cerrakin explodes with anger, I retaliate with a shower of words. "An eagle flies high above, and is not rummaging in the pigeon loft like an oversized badger, evil cat or a mutant rat on a killing spree, and I know those three suspects seem highly unlikely, but I just mention them because I crossed them off my suspect list and an eagle was never on that list, we would have seen it and if it had a broken wing it still wouldn't go labyrinthing in The Vault, at least I wouldn't have swapped the entire sky with a dark and gloomy maze, and if I did I wouldn't kill in such numbers to raise suspicion and Starion found pigeons that had been killed but not so much as nibbled on, so that is evil killing and therefore they are not doing it for food, but for stopping messages getting through to us and that means we probably have a suspect here among us, maybe not for the killing itself but for setting it up and that person zapped me on purpose."

"That was a handful," Cerrakin says, "but lucky for you, Miss Huckerpucker, I was actually listening. So who is your suspect?"

"Hm, I haven't had time to dwell on that," I say, but then a clue comes to mind. "I got a one hinged zap!"

"Which means?"

"It must be a four hinger! After all, you demoted me to a three hinger. And before that you demoted me to a four hinger."

"That leaves you out of the suspect list then," Cerrakin says sarcastically. "And you haven't explained the eagle's appearance."

"It was a construct."

"A construct?"

"Made by magic, the same way I made Tenderloin by accident."

"And how did you do that?"

"I mostly didn't," I confess. "It ate a lucky charm, a rabbit's foot to be exact. And I found a rabbit's foot in the eagle's chest, pierced by a dagger. I think Crazyjones killed the construct, but we still have to deal with the traitor among our ranks who has been supervising it.

"What thrilling evidence!"

"Thank you."

"And you say it must be a four hinger?"

"Yes."

"Well, there are no four hingers in The Vault. They all left with Donnowan Dragonslayer, together with all the five hingers."

"What about the archivists?" I ask.

"Only three hingers and less."

"But who is studying my skeletal hand then?" Then it dawns on me. "That's the reason you demoted me! You wanted the skeletal hand for yourself, Cerrakin!"

"No," he protests, but looks like a small kid caught red-handed.

"Yes, you did!"

"I… didn't want you to blow up The Vault with your exploratory spelling."

"Exploratory spelling!" I shout and stand up, leaning over the table. "That exploratory spelling brought the whole hand here intact. Who else has ever done that?"

Cerrakin cringes from my accusations and he doesn't call on Ol'Blindeye to sit me down in the chair, so I know I have found a soft spot – his guilty conscience – and I'll keep drilling into it.

"Was it for the same reason you sent Donnowan and all the four and five hingers on an impossible mission up in the Peccaran Lands?"

"No, no!"

"But you wanted them out of the picture, didn't you? You knew there was a big bone coming, you saw it in that crystal ball of yours, and you wanted that bone all to yourself," I say, since we both know that I know that he has an affinity for seeing into the future – quite handy when you are a boss – and that it for some strange reason doesn't work very well on me. I barged in on him once when he was crystal ball gazing – that was when I was a five hinger and could go through his door unannounced – and learnt his affinity with future predictions by accident. I have never revealed that affinity of his to anyone. It is probably only me and Ol'Blindeye that knows this.

"The mission in the Peccaran Lands is real, Miriam."

"But you sent them away on purpose."

His shoulders slump and I know I have won the first skirmish, but the war is far from won. The way his child hands are grabbing at the edge of the table and his eyes roaming around in the office, means that he is looking for a respite, and I'm not going to give him one, I have to batter him while I have the chance.

Go for it, Mirry! I think to myself.

But then someone knocks on the door.

"Enter!" Cerrakin says, and releases his grip on the table and exhales in relief.

Chapter 39

Mabel Bytheway enters and closes the door behind her.

"You wanted to see me, Cerrakin?" she asks, putting on an innocent smile. She is hastily dressed and yawns like she's on stage.

Cerrakin and I glance shortly at each other, both of us suspicious, but neither of us saying anything. Without a word, we have agreed to a ceasefire.

At least I hope so.

"Please sit down," Cerrakin says.

Mabel sits down on a chair next to me, giving me the hi-so-nice-to-see-you-expression, which is not like her at all, but I nod and put on my best nice-to-see-you-here-too- expression in turn.

"Do you know why you are here?" Cerrakin says.

Mabel nods. "The menace in the pigeon loft has been dealt with. And I must compliment Miss Huckerpucker on finding such a good candidate."

"Thank you," I say.

"We are all happy on that account," Cerrakin assures her, "but I have some questions about working hours. I know that you are so concerned with the well being of The Vault's workers and the safety regulations, so I would like to hear from you, not Miss Huckerpucker here, an explanation as to why poor Crazyjones worked in the middle of the night and was not supervised, seeing as you yourself demanded supervision from Curan the moment you got here. I also think you came right here now from his supervising, or maybe it was the other way around. You are after all both three hingers, actually Curan is soon to be four, so none of you should need any supervision."

Mabel Bytheway actually reddens. Her eyes dart around, but I refrain from eye contact, and she ends up looking at her feet when she offers her explanation.

That is so me, I think.

It is strange to see another collector wriggle under Cerrakin's scrutinising gaze.

"He must have been inspired," Mabel says at last.

"Inspired?"

"Yes, when Crazyjones left work, he was pondering something. I guess he got a bright idea, like some people do," here she gives me a quick glance, "and ran back after hours to test out his theory."

"But you weren't there, were you?"

"Oh no, I would never let him work in the dark," Mabel assures him. "You know my stance on safety regulations."

You're only using them as excuses to skip work.

If Cerrakin is of a similar mind as me, he doesn't show it. Instead he smiles, making Mabel smile back, feeling let off the hook.

Of course she isn't. Being a good rule breaker – that is Tuddernut's term – I have been in Mabel's situation plenty of times, with Cerrakin hovering over me. Metaphorically speaking, that is. He is the actual size of an eight year old, and even propping him up on pillows doesn't give him the opportunity to look down on us much, not after a while anyway. The pillows he uses are soft and nice and start sagging after a few minutes.

Right now he is actually half a head shorter than us, and a full head shorter when he leans forward.

"Then, Miss Bytheway, I have only one question before you can leave."

"Yes?" she says and leans forward as well.

"How did poor Crazyjones manage to get into the pigeon loft?"

"He walked, I guess…"

"If he'd done that, he would have been zapped like Braidive, unless…" Cerrakin looks at us both now and lifts something dangling from a silvery thread. "…this three hinged necklace might explain matters?"

"Wow," I say and lean forward to look closer at the encasing with the faint shine of soul fire.

Mabel Bytheway looks instantly at her feet.

Only then do I understand that I have been ticked off of Cerrakin's list of suspects.

Chapter 40

It's awkward being a bystander and not on the receiving end of Cerrakin's anger. He unleashes all his fury upon Mabel, and she instantly breaks down in tears.

Before he continues I act stupid and step in between.

He is on his way to scold me as well, but is baffled when I say: "You can save it for later, you can scold me and I promise to last longer than poor Mabel Bytheway, she may be a slacker that deserves some scolding, but right now has to repent."

"Repent what?" she sniffles and turns to me.

Cerrakin is so out of tune and nonplussed with me doing anger management on him, and not the other way around, that he just lets me continue speaking.

"Mabel, do you really think Starion ran away?"

"Maybe."

"Why do you think that?"

"He said the place was haunted."

"The pigeon loft?" Cerrakin asks, having forgotten his anger.

Mabel nods but keeps her eyes at her feet while she talks. "He said there was a red eyed monster up there, but I thought he was pulling my leg."

"And what did Crazyjones say?"

"He didn't say anything," but the way she says it raises my suspicion.

Something is amiss.

"But did he do something out of the ordinary?"

"I can't tell," Mabel says and peers up at me. "Cerrakin is going to unhinge poor Crazyjones if I tell you. And maybe me in the process."

Smart move, Mabel.

I know she has gathered her wits somewhat, but I let her carry on playing crybaby, and discreetly look at Cerrakin.

Come on! I think, knowing that my thoughts are often on full display on my face.

He nods discreetly back and says in a soothing voice: "I promise not to unhinge you, Mabel. So what did Crazyjones do?"

Mabel sniffles loudly and then spills the beans. "He came down with a lot of pigeon tubes."

"From where?" asks Cerrakin, suddenly impatient.

"The tubes had markings from the Northern Territories and Donnowan's expedition."

From there everything accelerates to lightning speed. Mabel is instantly grounded or jailed or whatever you wish to call Ol'Blindeye manhandling her and stuffing her wrapped up and gagged into a closet, while Cerrakin and I sprint over to the pigeon loft.

When he starts to run down the corridor, I stop him.

"What?"

"Let's diminish and go through here," I say and point at a ventilation hole in the wall.

We both go "Gelly-golly-fith-la-folly-umbun-da!" and our diminished selves run up a sloping air shaft and when we exit we both cry "Yerra-yerra-dubboli-dub-derram-dwinklehood- astar-yep-sturry!" and grow big again, which is quite small compared to other people.

The shortcut saves us time and we arrive at the three hinged door to the pigeon loft where Mister Hunt is on guard duty. He might be shrivelled and ugly, but he is courteous and nice and opens the door for us without questions, and closes it afterwards when we enter the pigeon loft like two detectives from one of the books in the Coffee Shop Mysteries series.

"Nothing has been touched since we found you and Crazyjones here, except for him," Cerrakin says and points to a pigeon cage. Inside sits a whimpering Tenderloin, but he starts to bark and wag his tail when he sees me.

"Mind if I let him out? He did a good job finding the crime scene."

"Waking the whole Vault you mean?" Cerrakin asks, but then he nods. "Keep him on a short leash. I don't want him eating evidence. Or pissing on it for that matter."

I promise to keep him close and when I walk to the cage his tail wags so vigorously against the netting that it sounds like a drunken troubadour harassing a lute. He barks and is overjoyed when I pick him up and also seems satisfied to be leashed, at least as long as he is leashed to me.

"Help me with the overturned table, Miriam," Cerrakin says. "The tubes must be in Mabel's drawer."

"If nobody's stolen them," I add, but I see that the thought has also crossed his mind.

Together we lift the table, while Tenderloin lifts his hind leg to do dog stuff on one of the table legs, but when nothing comes out, his ears go down and the tail stops wagging.

We pull out the drawer and rummage through the contents, finding at least two dozen small metal tubes, either with the markings from the Northern Territories or Donnowan's expedition.

"This is a disaster," Cerrakin says, even before he opens the first tube.

As I said, he is good at prediction.

It is a disaster. The small messages convey that Donnowan has gone missing, probably killed or captured up in Peccaran Lands, which seems like good news compared to the rest of it, a list of confirmed deaths caused…

"…by a dragon", Cerrakin reads, then slumps down in Mabel's chair. Without the pillows he looks really small, especially with his legs dangling in the air.

While he despairs – he seems like a natural – I read through the rest of the tubes. I'm used to being in trouble, so even though it is disturbing to read of the misfortune of others, I try as I always do, to see the situation from the bright side.

This is as bright as a midwinter morning, actually quite bleak.

I imagine Donnowan being spit-roasted by hungry Peccarans and the other four and five hingers being burnt to cinders or sliced to pieces by sharp talons, and if not gobbled up instantly, coated with Peccaran hoarfrost and stored for later consumption by a voracious dragon.

The last part is actually from the Coffee Shop Mysteries and though I at first found it imaginative – having a dragon in the freezer in the back room – I later found it highly unlikely and then I couldn't believe in the story and –

"Miriam?"

I look up. Cerrakin has regained some of his composure.

"Yes, Vault Master?"

"Who are the survivors?"

I ruffle through the messages. "It seems that Slyslink, Enjin and Lilly Fairhair are alive at least."

"Slyslink, the worst five hinger ever," Cerrakin sighs.

Wait, isn't that me?

Then I remember that I have been demoted to three hinges.

"And the troublesome twins," he adds. "How much time has passed since that last message?"

The bleak winter morning in my head brightens.

"Not more than a week," I say.

"And how likely is it that they've survived the week?"

"You ask me?"

"You belong to the troublesome lot here," Cerrakin says with a faint smile. "You think like them. I do not. So what would you do in their situation?"

I ponder on that for a minute.

Slyslink has been fencing, selling and buying goods illegally for as long as I can remember, without Cerrakin ever noticing it, so he is probably stacked up with all sorts of goodies to defend himself. And the troublesome twins are both capable fighters, even better at teamwork and best at taking the shit out of anyone that crosses their path.

Snowfalls will be to their advantage as it will reduce the line of sight and blizzards is even better as that will keep the hostiles, who is basically everyone Peccaran, indoors and make it harder for a dragon to fly around in the air and take its pick of bone assemblers, as long as the weather doesn't get too cold as we assemblers can freeze to immobility – which is why I found the freezer to be scarier than the dragon in the Coffee Shop Mysteries – but my colleagues should be able to use campfires unseen as the Peccaran Lands are vast and sparsely inhabited with lots of dense forests, at least when you look at the map.

Since they don't have to worry about food and they have enough firewood on hand to counter the freezing, I count the desolation as an advantage as well.

As long as they don't make a bonfire out in the open, that is.

I keep that worry to myself and continue to look at it from the bright side.

"I reckon they could hold out for one to three months, tops."

Cerrakin nods and straightens up. "But first we have to deal with the traitor in our midst."

"So you believe me now?"

"I wish I didn't, but the evidence at hand refutes my earlier and hasty conclusions." He jumps down from the chair and walks over towards the rotting eagle carcass. "This bird has been long dead. And the rabbit's foot stuck to the dagger has been sizzled."

He picks up the dagger and points it at me so I can have a closer look at the foot. All the hairs have been burnt. And then he points the dagger at the ruptured eagle's chest. I bend down to have a look.

"You're right, Cerry," I say. "The chest is burnt on the inside. It looks like there has been a connection that has short circuited. It reminds me of…"

No, better forget that.

"…the time you exploded the roast pig in the kitchen and we all had to eat vegetarian on Christmas eve."

"That was a loooong time ago," I say in my defence, "and I thought I could cut down on the roasting time if I put that lucky charm – I actually bought that as a present for Tuddernut – inside the pig and–"

Cerrakin waves me off. "It doesn't matter. I want you to find the traitor, Miriam-style."

"You mean fast."
"And unconventional."
"Thanks," I say. Cerrakin is stingy with compliments. I decide that this is a compliment now that I am looking at things from the bright side.

He must be pretty desperate when he starts cooing at you, one of my sinister thoughts says. But I ignore it.
Mirry, mirry on the wall –
Snuck off!
The sinister thought leaves me, but promises to return.
"So how much time do I have?"
He raises three fingers.
"Three days? Then I'll first wake up Crazyjones and…"
"Not three days, Miriam," he says with a grave voice.
"Three… hours?"
He nods, all too serious.

Chapter 41

"Are you kidding me!"

"No." Cerrakin looks grim, far too grim for that child's face of his, and again his actual age seeps through his facade. "I'm not doing this to punish you, Miriam, but by my estimations three hours is all that we have, at the maximum, before word spreads throughout the dome of what has happened here."

"Wouldn't that be to our advantage?"

"Think, Miriam. When the traitor knows we're on his heels, he is either going to flee or to strike."

"And do you have an idea where he will strike?"

"If I was him, or her, I would go for a big skeletal hand, but first I would do some distracting sabotage to lead people astray." Cerrakin takes the rabbit's foot off of the dagger's pointy end and tucks it in a pocket. "Let's split. I will go and gaze in my crystal ball to look for clues, while you chase the bastard down. We rendezvous at my office in one hour and thirty minutes."

He gives me the sleek dagger which has a higher quality than our home forged swords, and that says a lot. Slyslink has been selling a couple of those swords with a considerable profit. I know this because he wanted me to lose my sword as well, after persuading the troublesome twins to lose theirs on a mission.

"Why should I have the dagger?" I ask.

"The dagger was in Crazyjones' possession, he had the sheath attached to his belt," Cerrakin says and hands me the sheath as well. "I think that he would prefer you to take care of it."

"I would prefer to have my sword instead," I confess.

"I know, but seeing you walking around with a sword would raise suspicion. After all, you are grounded, and grounded personnel are not allowed to strut around with weapons."

I'm not strutting!

But still I agree to just carry the dagger.

"And I want to borrow that three hinged necklace."

"Why?"

"You don't want to know, that is why you asked me to solve this." With a sigh, he hands me the necklace as well.

"And I want my two hinges back," I say and when I see he disagrees, I add, "unless you want me to get zapped going through a door with four or five hinges."

"It will take at least fifteen minutes to do that!"

I hold up three fingers, he understands all too well, and he does it in three minutes, but seems to be so annoyed and drained – the undead term for exhausted – that I skip demanding anything more, like enlarging Tenderloin to a more beastly size or borrowing Cerrakin's magic crown. I don't know if he has one, but the nickname King Kiddo has to come from somewhere and if he has a crown, it must be magic, him being so good at spelling. Cerrakin is the only nine hinger in the whole Vault, with Donnowan Dragonslayer as his only competitor at seven hinges. And since no one has six hinges, and apparently almost all the five hingers have been wiped out, me and Slyslink share third place – Ol'Blindeye doesn't count, he is super strange –, and if Slyslink is destroyed – the proper undead term for killed – I'm number three on the list of greatness.

Or maybe even number two, if Donnowan has been eaten by Peccarans.

"You have to survive," I say to Cerrakin. "I don't want to be number one!"

"I don't know what you are talking about," Cerrakin answers, "and prefer to keep it that way. I have unlived for a long time, so I'll unlive at least two hours and forty seven minutes more."

"I'll do my best," I say and run so fast through the door that I catch Mister Hunt reading the Earthy Soft Rose on the other side of the door. He has been hiding the book behind the shield while pretending to be on guard.

"Clever," I say.

"Not half as clever as you," he answers. "It's quite feisty."

"The book?"

"No, the dedication, be-cute-with-a-light-embrace," he says and in the same instant the book flies off his hand and hits me like a crossbow bolt.

Chapter 42

I buckle over from the punch of the book.

The last I see before being hit is a triumphant expression on Mister Hunt's shrivelled face.

So he is the traitor? That can't be!

Mister Hunt walks over to me, sword in hand, while I scramble for the dagger. But I'm too dazed to react fast enough.

"It worked," he says.

I'm trying to hit him with my right fist, but he grabs hold of it.

Now I'm dead, real dead, I think, steeling myself for his upcoming sword thrust through my chest. I learnt the hard way, in Mister Hunt's gymnastic classes, that impaling the heart with a good sword thrust is one way of putting an undead on hold.

The other one is chopping the head off, something that both me and Flatface learnt when Mister Hunt sliced Flatface's head off like an overripe cabbage and it landed in my lap. I was his assistant teacher at that time.

And now you are his next murder victim.

I try to wrest free from Mister Hunt's grip, and wriggle as best I can to make my heart a difficult target, but instead of impaling me he hoists me up on my feet. Just as in the serials I read, he has to sputter some evil villain talk that will give me an advantage.

All hope is not lost.

"I'm sorry, very sorry, Miriam," he says and lets go of me. Then he bends over, picks up the book and blows dust from it, before handing it over to me.

"You are not going to kill me?"

"I stopped doing that a long time ago, but if you volunteer I'll gladly impale you in my class so the students' understand our undead mortality better.

"No thanks."

"Or you can stab me, that would be a good twist. I owe you that."

"Owe me?"

He nods vigorously, his leathery dry skin creaking. "That spell of yours is amazing."

"You mean the mule kick?"

"Yes. The spell is both simple and easy to learn." He smiles with all his shrivelled face, and the creaking makes it sound like I'm aboard an old sailing ship. "Why has never anyone thought of it before? Instead of the hogwash gibberish we say, you use a real sentence. So smart and refined. And we can throw them around in public without people knowing. Much, much better than the arcane incantation!"

I don't know what to say. I'm still dazed. And I also lost five more minutes on my countdown.

Mister Hunt gets it, since I'm not my usually over-enthusiastic self.

"Something is wrong," he says. "How may I help you?"

"I'm looking for a four hinger."

He looks up to his left side, his thinking stance I call it, and then looks back to me.

"Are you in a hurry as usual?"

"Yes."

"Then you will never reach any four hinger. Everyone is too far away from The Vault. On Donnowan's expedition."

"But there must be a four hinger in The Vault! I got zapped by one."

He frowns, not quite believing me. He has no problem believing I got zapped, or that I know the grade of it, but rather that it has to be a four hinger who did it.

"I was a four hinger once," he says eventually.

"And so was Tuddernut and Curan as well, but they both chose retirement."

Retirement we call it, when people try to get ticks on the disobedience track to be demoted. Three hingers are not allowed to go on solo missions, but usually stay in or near The Vault. Our Vault Master, Cerrakin, understood this a long time ago, so he demotes without fuss. Bone hunting is a dangerous business, so he only wants the willing and able, and when they grow tired or –

"I chose retirement only after I got to look like this," Mister Hunt says from afar while I'm thinking, mostly thinking I won't get anywhere.

"Hmpf."

"Pommy Phart was also a four hinger."

"Yes."

"So you knew?"

"No."

"And you are not listening, are you?"

"Hmpf."

He elbows me so hard that I return to reality.

"I would like to help you, but you have to give me something more to go on," Mister Hunt says. He straightens me up as he did in class when I was sulking, and looks me in the eyes. "Give me the facts."

"I got a one grade zap when I touched my protégé to see how badly he fared after he killed that carcass in there that had a rabbit's foot as a heart."

"Why was Crazyjones in there?"

"To get rid of the vermin killing off our pigeons."

"I get that, Miriam," he says. "But why was he there in the middle of the night? Who let him through that three hinged door?"

Just as me, Mister Hunt can't imagine Mabel Bytheway working overtime, no matter how dire the circumstances are.

And right now they are dire.

"This necklace let him through the three hinged door," I say and lift up the silvery necklace.

"Those reinforcer necklaces don't only do that, you know," he says and study it closely. "They also reinforce the spelling of the caster."

"So if my Crazyjones, I mean mine as he is my protégé –"

"Get to the point."

"If he did spelling during the fight at the pigeon loft, he did it as a three hinger, because of the necklace?"

"In that you are correct, Miriam Huckerpucker."

"Then I need to find a reinforcer necklace that is four hinges strong."

"And I know one is in circulation."
"How so?"
"It was stolen from my drawer in the teachers' lounge."

Chapter 43

"Where are you going?" Mister Hunt says, when I tuck my Earthy Soft book inside the jacket – it actually gives me a bosom and an idea for what to wear on the next undeadly ball – and I turn to walk down the corridor towards the teachers' lounge.

"Have you changed the password?" I ask over my shoulder.

"We have been planning to change–"

"–it next month." I turn around. "You have been saying that for years."

Mister Hunt looks as guilty as a corpse can look.

But it's not his fault, a tender thought of mine insists, then a more angry one approaches and thinks: *I bet it must be Mabel Bytheway that has been stalling the change of password on the door. She sits there and footsies with Curan while the rest of the teachers drone about all the plans they never realise. If they actually did do something, the teachers' planning and discussion board would quickly run out of things to do.*

I bet Mabel invented the teachers' board to skimp real work, a third thought says and starts mixing and discussing with the other two.

"Miriam?" Mister Hunt says loud enough to bring me back to reality. He knows my habit of zoning out.

"Thanks," I say, and then ask, whispering, "is the password still 'Don't eat breakfast the day you die'?"

He affirms with a discreet nod and a "Happy hunting."

"Thanks."

"If you happen to find a small wooden playing piece, it's probably mine. I lost one of the towers from my chess game."

"I'll put it in your drawer if I find it," I say and turn around the corner. As soon as Mister Hunt is out of sight, Tenderloin reappears at my side.

"Where have you been?"

"Woof!"

That doesn't make me any wiser.

149

"Were you afraid of Mister Hunt?" I ask.

"Woof!"

I'll take that as a yes.

"Everyone is afraid of Corpsy in the beginning," I explain to Tenderloin. "That's what we call Mister Hunt when he is not around. You'll get used to him."

"Woof!" The little beast barks and wags its tail.

"But now I need your help to find something," I say and look down at Tenderloin. The little beast raises its ears. "We have to find a clue. Will you help me?"

I interpret a "Woof!" and vigorous tail wagging as a yes.

"But I don't know what the clue is, and we only have two and half hours left."

"Woof!" the dog barks.

We run along the corridors and five minutes later we are in front of the five hinged door to the teachers' lounge. The spell put on the door is simple. If you say the right password, two of the hinges disappear. I learned that the hard way, having obtained the password when I was a one hinger, saying the password and strolling through like I had done it and then getting a second grade zap and a visit to the mortuary.

I lift up Tenderloin so he will pass with me, enclosed in my aura. I don't know how doors affect him, and I'm not about to find that out now.

"Don't eat breakfast the day you die," I say, and in the same instant I say it I remember that I didn't need the password as I am back on five hinges, not three, and walk through the door.

I get a tingling sensation when I go through the doorway, like the door is checking if I'm worth zapping, something it definitely shouldn't do when it is three hinged and I'm a five hinger.

Strange.

I put Tenderloin down on the carpeted floor, before making a closer inspection of the door. Tenderloin runs straight to the lounging part with the soft couches, but he doesn't jump up, but wriggles himself under a two seater.

I hope he finds something of interest.
At least I do. Some kind of clue. The door still has five hinges and doesn't respond to the password.
Someone has changed the password recently.
That is a perfect sabotage distraction, zapping a teacher on the way into the teachers' lounge.
It must be the traitor.
Then I realise something else.
Silence.
"Tenderloin?"
No response.
The last I saw of him was when he ran under that couch.
I put a hand on my dagger and approach silently, but I'm feeling watched. Instead of being stupid and looking under the couch, I'm stupid and say "Be-cute-with-a-light-embrace!"
The couch blows into the stone wall and shatters with a tremendous crash.
The hooded person under the couch is taken by surprise and releases Tenderloin, but too late I understand that is intentional – a distraction – when the figure with lightning reflexes dodge sideways, picks up a big candlestick on the way and swings it at me.

Chapter 44

I draw my dagger to parry.

The candlestick stops an inch from the blade.

"That dagger is mine," a female voice under the hood says.

I recognize the sharply curved jaw line from all the wanted posters that used to be plastered on every wall.

"Erina Bulchec?"

"Or Raithea," she says, but draws the hood back now that the game is up. She lowers the candlestick, but her eyes are locked on the dagger I hold. "That dagger is mine," she repeats.

I have always liked her, well, what the gossip has said about her, so I am in awe, but at the same time I remind myself that she is a one hinger and I have five hinges, so I have to be the bossy one.

"How did you get in?"

"Give me my dagger and I'll tell you."

"This dagger is worth a lot more than that," I say to gain time while I scrutinise her. She has sawdust on her shoulders, big chunky bits.

I give her a knowing smile. "You drilled a hole through the roof and diminished yourself, didn't you? Isn't that what they teach you first in spelling class?"

"How did you know?"

"The sawdust. You enlarged them as well when you resized," I say matter-of-factly. "Next time brush off the sawdust, before you do the swelling."

"Thanks," Raithea says, "but that is still my dagger. How did you come by it?"

"It impaled the beast next to Crazyjones."

"Crazyjones? What happened to him?"

"He was attacked in the pigeon loft. Your dagger saved him," I say, and I really want to give it back, but I also really need to find a traitor in two hours time or thereabout. "I'll keep the dagger as evidence as long as his case is pending…" I say and leave it like that.

"But?" she says.

"But what?" I reply.

"I know that look," Raithea says with a sly smile. "You are willing to give me the dagger, but you want something back."

"Okay. I'm looking for a clue."

"What?"

"I don't know. Something out of the ordinary."

"Apart from that we are all undead?" she says and puts the big candlestick down on the table, and sits down to give Tenderloin a cuddle. When she scratches him behind the ear, his tail drums happily against the floor.

"You already found something, haven't you?"

"I might," she says and strokes the little beast's stomach now that he has rolled over and has his tongue hanging out of his mouth. Then she looks up at me with a serious expression. "But we don't have much time with all the noise you made."

Oh shit.

She is right. The couch is kindling and feathers. It looks like a woodshed has collided head on with a henhouse.

"I'll strike a deal with you, Erina Bulchec."

"Raithea please, I'm supposed to be incognito. The new name is a part of a witness program or something like that, to keep me safe from harm."

You seem to be doing a good job getting into harm's way.

"Raithea then," I say. "Here is my deal. I'll take the blame for the collateral damage–"

"Well, you did the couch killing, so why shouldn't you?"

"–and I leave you out of the story. But then I want you to put all the things you stole back where they belong."

"And my dagger?"

"You'll get the dagger when you give me a clue," I say and sheath the dagger and hide it back inside my jacket, under my new strutting bosom, also known as Earthy Soft.

"I'm not shaking hands on that, but let's start dealing," Raithea says and empties her pockets. There is a lot of jewellery and trinkets and two pigeon tubes and also a tower chess piece.

"Where did you find that?"

"The tower chess piece? Under the couch actually."

"No, I meant these tubes," I say and pick them up. They both have the markings from Donnowan's expedition.

This is suspicious. Why would anyone hide them here?

"I found them in that drawer." Raithea points at Mister Hunt's working desk, where cloth and grindstones and fighting manuals have been put up like pieces on a chess board.

"No that can't be right," I say. "He would never hide messages like that."

"I knew there was something off, when I found them," Raithea says and her eyes gleam like green jewels.

"How so?"

"They were haphazardly hidden and…"

"…and what?"

"You give me my dagger and I tell you something more."

I give in and give her the dagger.

"Both tubes dewed."

"I don't understand."

"Like a cold glass of lemonade. You know when the waiter serves you that on a hot sunny day, it doesn't take long before the glass forms dew on the outside."

"So they were brought here from somewhere cold? Like the pigeon loft?"

"Could be."

But that doesn't make sense. Unless the traitor… of course! He was there when the fight between the flying beast and Crazyjones took place. He placed the spell on Crazyjones that zapped me. And he did it with the four hinger necklace he stole from Mister Hunt. Then he ran here and put the pigeon tubes in Mister Hunt's drawer to throw us off the scent and use Mister Hunt as a red herring, and at the same time cause a big ruckus by changing the password.

To change the password he must know it already.

I look up at Raithea and ask while reviewing my mental suspect list, "Where is Flatface?"

He might only have one hinge left but with a four hinged reinforcer necklace he could do more havoc than when he had his three hinges intact.

"Flatty is in the mortuary. Selina Sekunda didn't have time to revive him, she is still working on Braidive and her second grade zapping."

"You know this for sure?"

"Sheet-Owl has been down there looking to Braidive, and he is not a liar and has no reason to lie, so yes, I'm sure." Raithea cocks her head sideways. "You are going through a checklist, aren't you? I use to do that when it comes to inventory."

"Then you can help me."

"Why?"

"The password to the teachers' lounge has been changed recently by a traitor."

"That sounds serious," Raithea says, then decides. "I'll help you. I hate people ratting."

"And the password has been changed in the last few hours."

"Then you can tick Timeon Flatface off your list. And Selina Sekunda as well, she hasn't left the mortuary, according to Sheet-Owl, who I trust."

I tick them off my list mentally.

"You can also tick off Mister Hunt, because someone tried to plant evidence on him."

Tick.

"Who else is on your list?"

"Curan, Tuddernut and Pommy Phart."

"Curan has already left The Vault."

"How do you know?"

"The pigeon lady told me that to my face in a not too friendly fashion. She thinks that I'm in love with her stevedore man," she says and gives me another of her sly smiles.

"How did you know he worked at the docks?" I ask. I know Curan is not proud of his past, so he hides it.

"I recognized his tattoos, Miriam. They all have it at the docks. I grew up there," she says and rolls up one of her sleeves.

Very tattooed indeed.

I'm especially fascinated by the sea serpents and krakens that coil around a tankard of ale on her bicep, with a ship on top and sea maidens swimming in the ale under it.

"I thought you were a noble lady gone thieving."

"I like people to think that," Raithea says and rolls back her sleeve.

"So what did Mabel Bytheway do to you?"

"Bothered me. But she ran off screaming when I implied to Lady Pigeon that I have had plenty of time to view Curan's tattoos from top to bottom."

"That was evil."

"No, it was just. She started the fight. I ended it. Verbally. Not lethally."

"Well, she deserved her nose snubbed," I say and return to the investigation. "Tuddernut and Pommy Phart?"

"Can't help you there." She turns to the small hoard on the table. "But you can help me pick one from here."

"You promised not to steal."

"I have to have proof that I have been here. Me and Gorth have a wager going. And I'm not going to lose."

I look at the small hoard on the table. Then I pick up the tower chess piece.

"Put everything back where you found it, using your mental inventory list, and then put the tower piece you found under the couch, together with the other pieces on Mister Hunt's chess board and challenge him to a game with you tomorrow. He will be very surprised to find no pieces missing."

"Clever. That will work as proof." Raithea looks at the door. "But how are you going to keep people out? Someone must have heard the couch crashing to cinders. And I have plenty to put back according to my mental checklist.."

"You have some time while I deactivate the door," I tell her and walk over to the five hinged door.

As a five hinger I can pluck off the hinges of a door up to my level. I really don't have the time, but I consider it necessary to take two of the hinges off so none of my colleagues are zapped.

"In the meantime, you stand guard at the perimeter," I say to Tenderloin. He wags his tail, and trots off to a corner in the corridor.

At first I am amazed that he understands, but then I see he lifts his hind leg, trying again to mark territory. He continues doing doggy business while I reduce the door from five to three hinges.

That will do.

When I look inside, Raithea is long gone, and so is a lot of my time as well.

Then I remember the meeting I was going to have in one and a half hours with Cerrakin in his office.

I'm already too late, I feel it in my bones.

Chapter 45

Both Tenderloin and I arrive panting at the five hinged door to Cerrakin's office.

I regain my breath – actually I don't, but it is a habit I never managed to shake off and I intend to keep. People tend to be sceptical when they realise you don't breathe. And it is not good for your vocal cords either, you will sound rusty and raspy, and that will do you no good if you try to blend in as I like to do when I'm out on missions.

I knock on the door.

No answer.

I sigh – also a habit from my previous life – and then I open the door. I'm a five hinger now, I can walk straight in if I want to.

Cerrakin sits in his chair, staring at the roof like he is stargazing instead of ball gazing. The crystal ball lies on the floor like a discarded football, next to Ol'Blindeye, or his head to be correct. Cerrakin's manservant has been beheaded.

What the...

"Cerrakin!" I shout.

No reaction. Cerrakin has been pierced by a thin projectile that has lodged his small child body to the backrest of his chair.

On the pedestal the bone that my sword penetrated sputters soul fire from the wound my sword gave it.

The sword itself is gone.

And the soul fire has already eaten a good part off a nearby rug and is licking hauntingly up and down a tree pillar. Someone is trying to set fire to The Vault.

This is bad, I think. Then another more helpful thought says *Calm down and assess the situation.*

Thank you, thought.

And don't rush it, please. Neither further into the room or with the thinking.

Okay.

I assess. Someone must have shot Cerrakin as the door opened, creating a loud noise on impact, which made Ol'Blindeye turn to Cerrakin, which gave the assailant time to retrieve my sword from the bone and behead Ol'Blindeye, and then they – my sword and the assailant – probably left, planning to let the leaking bone engulf the crime scene and the victims.

See? That wasn't so hard was it?

No, it wasn't. Even if I think the assailant has escaped I step into the room warily, not looking too much at the bluish flame or the strange shine it casts on the surroundings.

I gingerly lift up the crystal ball in the hope that Cerrakin has left me some kind of vision, but there's only a swirling mist inside the translucent stone.

Then I hear a muffled voice nearby. Tenderloin also sharpens his ears.

"We are not alone," I whisper. I am holding the crystal ball ready to throw it, having no other weapons after giving Raithea her dagger back.

The sound comes from the closet.

Silly me!

I put down the crystal ball and open the closet where I find a gagged and bound Mabel Bytheway.

I remove the gag.

"What happened?"

"I don't know. I heard crashing and trashing," she says and then she sees Ol'Blindeye beheaded and Cerrakin impaled on a steely bolt. "Oh my god, what happened?"

"A traitor happened. And I want to know where he went."

Mabel holds out her bound hands. "Please release me, Miriam. I'm too old for this."

"You must have picked up something useful," I say. I'm not releasing her yet. When I pretend to consider closing the closet again, her mind suddenly starts working at full capacity.

"I know where the assailant went. I can show you."

I release her and help her out of the closet. She shakes her head at

the soul fire slowly consuming the office and the grisly crime scene.
"This is bad," she says to herself. "I need Curan."
"You need to tell me where the traitor went!" I say and shake her.
"You have no right –"
"I'm back on five hinges!"
"Oh." She acknowledges defeat and I let her go. "I'll show you."
She walks over to the closet and when she pushes it aside I can see that its legs are on wheels.
Behind the closet is a four hinged door.
So that is where you have kept my giant skeletal hand, Cerrakin.

Chapter 46

I order Mabel Bytheway to put out the soul fire and then call for help, not the other way around, and I also promise to couple Curan and Raithea if I find her results wanting when I come back.

If I come back, that is.

I leave Mabel to her task and walk in with Ol'Blindeye's sword in hand. It is a notch too heavy for me, but it is better than nothing. If need be, I can swing it with both hands.

The passageway leads – as I suspected – to the laboratory, where only four hingers and above are allowed. It is in semi-darkness, rows of bottles and boxes of stored ingredients filling the wall on each side and also sectioning off the different parts of the room. It reminds me of a deserted beehive somehow.

I wish Crazyjones –

Thump-thump.

Okay, better not think of him right now, considering the circumstances.

Thump-thump.

That is not my heart.

Tenderloin looks to the side and growls.

A man-sized shape thump-thumps behind a section of storing shelves and disappears from view.

Thump-thump as in knock on wood, or wood on wood in this peglegged instance.

There's only one person that could be!

"Pommy Phart! I know it is you!"

"I'm impressed," she cackles from behind the shelves. "You are a good thinker when you're not playing at being Cerrakin's lapdog."

"What do you mean?" I ask and sneak in a big circle around the section.

"He spared you from Donnowan's mission," she says loudly, trying to hide that she is working on something mechanical behind the shelves.

"What are you doing?"

"Releasing the skeletal hand."

That makes me jump into action. Raising my sword I turn the corner, and stop instantly.

The big skeletal hand is there, as Pommy Phart insinuated, but still nailed firmly to the wall, its fingers clawing air.

Pommy Phart is in front of me with her wooden leg detached. She is pointing it at me, glaring at me with spectacle-enlarged eyes.

"I had planned to let the dragon creature devour you, but your protégé killed it off."

"And you killed Starion."

"He was better off not existing, my dear, after his love went under the wheel."

"You killed Fernina!"

"Indeed." She cocks the wooden leg and a metallic bow springs out to the sides.

"A crossbow," I say more to myself than to her.

"No. This is better. It is a harpoon gun," she says with a smile that shows off her two golden front teeth. "Consider this payback for the dragon."

She aims at my chest.

"Wai–"

The harpoon hits me with such power that I'm flung at the wall behind me. Everything darkens, and I hear her whistle a jolly tune, from the time she worked as a pirate.

She limps over to me, but then Tenderloin goes into action.

Chapter 47

A few moments pass before I return from my knockout. I'm not dead, only bruised and dazed, with a pierced bosom. My new bosom saved me. It is still strutting, even when impaled. I take out the Earthy Soft book and look at it.

The harpoon almost got to the end of the book, only twenty or so pages to go.

It still hurts like hell when I try to get on my feet.

Luckily, Pommy Phart has no eyes for me.

Tenderloin is going crazy on her, snapping at the only leg keeping her aloft and tugging her clothes and shaking his head in an attempt to unbalance her. She loses her harpoon-gun-wooden-leg when she has to steady herself with both hands instead of toppling over, but then she regains some balance, and with one hand on the shelf and the other one drawing my sword – my very sharpened and oiled and cherished sword – she takes a swipe at Tenderloin.

NO WAY!

"BE-CUTE-WITH-A-LIGHT-EMBRACE!" I shout and think of ten thousand miles of kicking.

As I'm back on five hinges, Pommy Phart is flung with such power that parts of her trousers tear off and remain in Tenderloin's locked jaws, but the sword is still in her grip after slamming into the wall big time.

Even with the power of the mule kick, she is still conscious, and infuriated. She screams, leaning against the wall. "I will kill you!"

No, you won't.

I aimed with my mule kick.

Then she realises she is not leaning on the wall, but is in the embrace of the big skeletal hand.

"My master –"

She gets to say no more as the fingers envelop her body like giant white spider legs and crush her like a bug.

Her spectacles slump to the ground, broken.

Then I slump to the ground, drained.

Epilogue:
Chapter 48

Crazyjones wakes up in the mortuary, having no idea how long he has been dormant, but when he wakes up, it is with a cheer.

The cheer originates from the other one hingers, well, mostly from Gorth Northman, who also slaps him so hard that Crazyjones almost falls off the stone slab he has been lying on.

"How long have I been out?"

"Nine days," Selina Sekunda says and parts through Crazyjones' overenthusiastic classmates. She turns her sickly face to look at them. "That will be enough for today's reviving class. Off you go," she says and shoos them away.

"I'll be back," Raithea promises him.

"No distract," Gorth Northman says before he scampers off with rest of the class.

"No distract?"

"I think he means to say that his and all the others' disobedience track has been cleared," Selina says while mixing a concoction on the table next to Crazyjones. Then she hands it to him. "Drink this."

"What is it?"

"You don't want to know really, but you will revive faster."

Crazyjones drinks it.

"It tastes like sticky mud water," he says and swipes his mouth afterwards. "Nine days you say? I must have been pretty beat up."

"Luckily for you, the beast only slammed into your pulpy chest. If it had gotten the chance to tear at you with its claws or fangs your story would have ended. Permanently. Anyway, I also had to revive the Vault Master first."

Vault Master revival? That doesn't sound good, not good at all.

"What happened?" he asks.

"The usual," Selina Sekunda replies while cleaning the cup he drank from. "Miss Huckerpucker got to be in charge of the investigation after you got killed while ousting a small dragon that had been preying on our pigeons. In proper Miriam fashion, she took the meaning of the word 'charge' quite literally. She smashed the teachers' lounge, partly burned down the Vault Master's office and crushed one of the teachers to bits in the big skeletal hand she found."

No, no, no.

"So she has been put down for good?"

"No, the exact opposite. She has earned another hinge, making her just a hinge below Donnowan Dragonslayer. And he earned his seventh by killing a dragon up north. Now she heads the same way."

"You sound happy for her."

"That is just me being egotistical," Selina Sekunda says. "She is heading off to rescue the rest of Donnowan's expeditionary forces, and hopefully finding Donnowan himself."

"So you are happy that she is leaving?"

"Exactly." Selina Sekunda smiles so the corner of her mouth is filled with black foam. "And I'm not the only one. Gorth Northman is over himself with joy, now that he can return to the Peccaran homelands and show off his undead skill set and Raithea has also been accepted into Miriam's expeditionary force, along with Mister Hunt and some other proficient unfortunates. They have all been handpicked by her."

She is leaving.

Crazyjones is feeling… empty, while Selina Sekunda chatters on.

He tries to rise, but Selina tucks him back on the stone slab.

"You have to revive," she says sternly. "That means reading or recuperating."

"I don't know how to recuperate! I haven't learned it!"

"I will show you how. You can start by getting real drowsy, and have a flick through that book."

Next to him lies a pierced Earthy Soft book on the stone slab. It is buckled, like someone has stuffed it in a bag or something.

Selina rises and smiles.

"You can start with the dedication," she says.

Selina turns the wick up so the oil lamp turns the mortuary almost bright, and then she leaves.

Crazyjones opens the book and reads the dedication.

"Congratulations on killing the dragon in the pigeon loft and earning a hinge."

What?

"Am I a second hinger?" he shouts after Selina.

"Yes, you are. Cerrakin himself bestowed it on you. It was quite a ceremony, almost caused as much commotion as when she sailed in with you on that skeletal hand of yours."

And I passed out on both occasions.

Crazyjones continues reading to himself.

"I don't know what to write really, but I think you are –" the word has been crossed out, and another on top of that has been cross out, and another above that one again, all unreadable "– and I would appreciate it if you and Tenderloin (I have taken good care of him by the way) would join me on an expedition north. There are rumours that Donnowan's dragon is not dead at all and you are the only real dragonslayer we have, but I just made that up as an excuse (don't tell me that I wrote that!). Anyway I would really like if you would come along..."

There is more text on the page, but he is distracted by a small butterfly she has drawn, and when he looks closer it looks more like a heart that she has tried to hide.

Thump-thump.

And he smiles.

Peek: A few days into the future
Chapter 49

"You better look to the old belcher, son," his father says when dawn is just a few hours away. "And then get some sleep so you are fit for class tomorrow."

Jim Wise nods. He knows better than to argue when his father is in the closing-mood, and he has been in that mood for a while. You can see it by the rough way he swipes the tables and the fast way he refills the oil lamps.

Even if they earn good coin on the long-drinkers, it reduces their sleep and a good sleep is just as important as good money.

The old belcher is half asleep, eyes closed, snoring instead of belching and mumbling one of his good stories. The fact that everyone else at the table has left a long time ago is none of his concern. His stories live on in his wrinkled and liver-spotted head that Jim Wise thinks looks like a mouldy-haired raisin, mostly mouldy-haired around his ears, neck and mouth.

"It is past closing time," Jim Wise announces when there is a short break in the old belcher's drowsy mumblings.

The old belcher opens his reddish eyes and says, "and she was about your size, no, a few sizes smaller, but at your age." He puts a hand on Jim Wise's shoulder to partly lean and partly sag in on him.

Please don't go slobbering on me, Jim Wise thinks, and squints his eyes and closes his mouth to a thin strip when the old drunkard showers him with saliva, bad breath and the stench of alcohol as he continues to talk.

"How old are you, girl?"

"I'm eight. And NOT a girl."

"Hm," the old belcher murmurs, shakes his head and gets a clearer look in his eyes. "She was five I think. Maybe six. And she was no higher than your shoulder."

About the same size as wide-eyed Vinni.

Jim Wise clears his throat when he hears his father bang an upended stool onto a table, making it clear that they are way past closing time.

"You have to leave, sir."

"Of course, of course," the old belcher says. "Could you be my eyes to the door?"

"Yes, sir," Jim Wise says, but he sags down when the old belcher puts his full weight on Jim Wise's shoulders to get up. The drunkard sways like a tree in a storm, but with Jim as a crutch, he finds his balance and also the story that he continues while they zigzag through the tables and benches.

"She gave him a handkerchief."

"Who?"

"The little girl. She curtsied and presented herself as a true nobleman's daughter."

"And her name?"

"I don't remember her name, but the kerchief was embroidered with an M." The old belcher chuckles in his beard. "She said the M wasn't for Mini and one day she would be big and that she was quite big compared to her lapdog."

"She gave you a handkerchief?"

"No, you stupid wit! Aren't you listening? She gave it to my liege lord. And instead of being cruel, he was... amused?"

"Or maybe intrigued?" Jim Wise suggests as he unlatches the front door.

"Yes, intrigued would be a good word. At least I was intrigued when he took her kerchief to be her champion at the tournament."

"Did he win?"

"No. But later on he said it was worth it. I think he liked being a champion for someone so small who also had the audacity to approach him. And who didn't treat him like shit."

Jim Wise opens the door to the night outside. The cold breeze that meets them seems to wake up the old belcher somewhat, for he makes one of his famous belching sounds that is met with barks in the night.

"That was better," the old belcher says and stretches his back so it creaks like an old ship at sea.

"Was your master powerful?" Jim Wise asks.

"Not powerful in your sense of the word, young man." The old belcher pats Jim's head in a grandfatherly way. "Timeon Blackheart was cruel and cunning. A robber knight. But that day the little girl made him into something else. Something…"

"…you should sleep on," Jim Wise suggests and gives the old belcher a light nudge out of the doorway. "Have a good night, sir."

"No, he was never a good knight," the old belcher replies. "Except at that tournament."

The old belcher disappears into a dark alley and Jim Wise locks the doors and then carries the two pails of food refuse to the pig in the backyard. The pig, still lean and small, wakes up with a grunt when Jim Wise empties the pails in his bin.

The pig is eating like it has no concerns in the world, but then the pig is oblivious that it is fattened in the backyard for a reason.

Jim Wise looks forward to bring wide-eyed Vinni here at the end of autumn when the pig will be big and fat and squeal in terror and the kids will squeal in delight when his father will hang it from its hind legs, slash its throat and unblood it.

Jim Wise fancies wide-eyed Vinni, but he also wonders if her eyes are able to pop out. Capsize has been very persistent that he once saw Vinni's left eye pop out and then she just tucked it in again like nothing had happened. Even if Capsize isn't the sharpest knife in the drawer, he has a poker face and is good at pulling legs.

Maybe my father will let me slash the pig's throat this year, Jim Wise thinks now that he has turned eight and heard from more than one adult that he behaves older than he looks.

He ruffles the little pig's stiff hackle while it noses through the refuse and thinks that Vinni will be happy when he gives her a blood sausage from the poor creature. His father is renowned for the best blood sausages in the city.

But then the pig suddenly stops eating and skulks off into a dark corner.

From the other side of the wall – which would be South Cobbler

Alley – he hears the low murmur of talk and nervous snorts of horses. A travelling band who wants to get ahead of dawn.

Interesting.

A vague scent of death, decay and dirt wafts by.

Undeads? No wonder the pig ran away.

Tickled with curiosity, Jim Wise climbs onto the wall, making sure not to stick his head up like an idiot, but peer through a crack in it.

Leading their horses, an armed band is walking by. Hooded. But as they walk past a night lantern the small silhouette in front turns around to hush on the others in the warband and the hood slides off.

It is the same girl that sailed in on the skeleton hand.

Jim Wise is not the only pair of eyes who sees that.

Cast (alphabetically)

Braidive: A new recruit to The Vault who is very into glamour spelling.

Dimly: Another new recruit to The Vault who is... dim?

Capsize: One of the pupils in the classes at the ruined shrine. Named after his captain father who disappeared on the ocean.

Cerrakin: The Vault Master in charge of The Vault and all the bone assemblers.

Crazyjones: Who used to be the farmer John Kraze until a sudden change of occupation.

Curan: Bone assembler in The Vault who is a reviver, and a teacher in mourning classes, but also does his stint of pigeon-duty.

Donnowan: Knight, dragon slayer and bone assembler who went missing up north.

Enjin: The dark-haired half of the troublesome twins who followed Donnowan up north.

Embereyes: The only dragon that has ever been sighted in real life. Very big. Very bad. Caused a lot of havoc in the Northern Territories until put down by Donnowan.

Fernina: Miriam's best friend, killed under suspicious circumstances.

Funix: A new recruit to The Vault who used to be a gutter rat, doing odds and ends at the cheaper side of town.

Gorth: A Peccaran barbarian recently in the service of The Vault as a recruit. Laughs a lot and talks in a sing-song fashion, sporting a silvery beard and mane of hair.

Jim Wise: A smart kid who attends classes and helps his father run an inn in the city.

Juicycrunch: Crazyjones' beaky hoe.

Lilly Fairhair: The fair-haired half of the troublesome twins who followed Donnowan up north.

Mabel Bytheway: Bone assembler who is in charge of the pigeon loft in The Vault, but somewhat workshy.

Miriam Huckerpucker: Bone assembler with a lot of second thoughts.

Mister Hunt: The skeletal swordmaster who teaches gymnastics and reads pulp literature on the side.

Nom: Kid attending the classes at the ruined shrine, but mostly picking his nose.

Old belcher: A drunkard at the inn run by the father of Jim Wise.

Ol'Blindeye: Cerrakin's trusted manservant, considered odd by everyone in The Vault, Miriam included.

Old rattler: A teacher with a lot of scroll containers containing… wisdom? At least one contains the map of the world (at the beginning of this book).

Pommy Phart: Peglegged and many spectacled teacher with golden front teeth who is an archivist in The Vault, but now is stepping in for Curan to do the mourning classes.

Raithea: Newly recruited to The Vault as bone assembler. Rumoured to be the famous burglar Erina Bulchec.

Selina Sekunda: Reviver in The Vault, looks like she has been recently poisoned.

Sheet-Owl: A scholarly type who just started working in The Vault as a recruit.

Slyslink: A five hinged bone assembler with a tarnished reputation and foggy morality.

Starion: A troubadour bone assembler who did his stint of pigeon loft duty but then disappeared.

Tenderloin: Crazyjones' special dog who tags along when his owner changes occupation.

Timeon Flatface: A serial knight turned into a bone assembler to most people's regret. When not causing collateral damage, he likes to puff on his pipe.

Tuddernut: Teacher in spelling classes, combining magic and feast in a practical way (unless mis-spelled).

Vinni: A girl who attends classes at the ruined shrine.

Printed in Great Britain
by Amazon